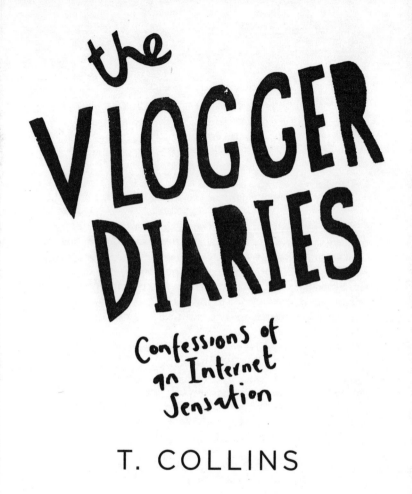

the VLOGGER DIARIES

Confessions of an Internet Sensation

T. COLLINS

Michael O'Mara Books Limited

First published in Great Britain in 2016 by
Michael O'Mara Books Limited
9 Lion Yard
Tremadoc Road
London SW4 7NQ

A CIP catalogue record for this book is available from
the British Library.

Papers used by Michael O'Mara Books Limited are natural, recyclable
products made from wood grown in sustainable forests.
The manufacturing processes conform to the environmental
regulations of the country of origin.

ISBN: 978-1-78243-617-1 in paperback print format
ISBN: 978-1-78243-618-8 in ebook format

1 3 5 7 9 10 8 6 4 2

Illustrations by Katie Abey

Designed and typeset by Envy Design Ltd

Printed and bound by CPI Group (UK) Ltd, Croydon, CR0 4YY

www.mombooks.com

ACKNOWLEDGEMENTS

Thanks to Jo Wyton, Fiona Slater,
Katie Abey, Anna Morrison and
everyone at Michael O'Mara Books.

MONDAY MARCH 27TH

HEY THERE WORLD! | THE DESTINY CHANNEL

Hey everyone! Destiny here! Welcome to my channel! I'm soooo excited to get started.

On this channel you'll see a whole bunch of stuff. I'm gonna show you my life and my shopping trips, how I do my makeup, my hair – this style is called the surfer-girl braid, by the way. I'll talk you through it in a minute …

But before that, there's someone else who I've just got to introduce you to. This is Loki. Isn't he the cutest? Say hi.

…

That was the start of my first ever vlog. Well, I say it was mine. I wrote the words, but I had to get a girl from school to perform them.

I tried recording a vlog of my own first. It wasn't good. I wrote it down, practised it in front of the mirror, and recorded it. Then I played it back. Ooh dear. Something had gone wrong. The voice coming out from my speakers was a flat, bored drawl. I swear my voice doesn't sound like that. My speakers were trolling me.

Also, I looked awful, like I'd just been woken up by a novelty ringtone at 4am. I decided I just wasn't very photogenic. Or microphone-genic. Or anything-genic. The Olivia Channel was not going to happen.

But I still wanted to make a vlog. I've always loved writing and creating things and, to be honest, I had discovered that top vloggers get loads of money from advertising. And I'd just found out there was an end-of-term school trip to New York I couldn't afford.

All I had to do was draw in a massive fanbase with

my winning personality, let them be bombarded with ads and grab my share of the profits.

Except my little test drive proved that my personality was more whining than winning and the only fanbase I was ever going to get was one that stopped my electric fan from falling over.

But then I thought of a clever way round it. I'd write the vlog, and get someone else to perform it. There's a girl at my new school called Emma, who did a dodgy advert for some sort of disgusting health milkshake. I don't think it ever came out in this country but she's always showing it on her phone.

In the ad, you see her smiling and swinging her hair next to a group of giggly girls, having an amazing time while slurping neon-coloured shakes. In fact they had to spit it into buckets between takes so they didn't end up spewing on to each other's shiny hair.

I talked her into doing my vlog by explaining it would be great exposure for her acting career. If she could play the role of deliriously happy girl with gross health drink, then friendly, chatty vlogger would be no problem. She agreed, but only after I promised to add £10 per video to the 'great exposure' she'd be getting.

Fine. If I had to invest what was left of my savings to make the vlog work, that's what I'd do. As soon as I got a fanbase, I'd double, triple, quadruple, whatever-the-next-word-is everything I put in.

Emma came round and recorded it this evening and it worked really well. She's really cliquey if you try and talk to her in school when she's with her gang The Swans (stupid name, I know), but she was great when we recorded. She came across like the ideal big sister you wish you had instead of your actual sister who keeps taking all your stuff without asking.

She even managed to improvise when my cat Loki jumped on to her lap and sniffed my keyboard. Loki's a pretty good actor too, come to think of it. He pretends he loves me five minutes before every mealtime.

I'm so excited about this vlog. I can concentrate on coming up with scripts, knowing that Emma will deliver them brilliantly. With my words and her acting, Destiny will become the perfect vlogger. Roll on the fandom and the profits.

TUESDAY MARCH 28TH

9AM

Right, I've uploaded the video. Just waiting for the view count to rise. I need it to take off fast because I've not got much of my savings left, and I don't want to use them all on Emma's fees.

6PM

Still waiting.

I know I need to be patient. Nothing goes viral right away. Even Sneezing Panda took a couple of months to catch on, and that's the greatest thing in the history of entertainment.

7PM

The vlog has only had 14 views so far, and I think most of them were me. And there's only been one comment:

> **$$$ BARGAINS $$$**
> Genuine designer sunglasses. 90% off. Last day of clearance. Click now! Fast shipping.

Hmm. Not a great start. Unless someone likes the vlog so much they really want to share sunglasses deals.

Come on, viewers, this is quality stuff. Why aren't you watching it?

8PM

21 views now, and a new comment:

Crafter101
OMG great video! Check out my channel <u>Crafter101</u>.

I got really excited when I read the bit about them liking the video, but I clicked through to Crafter101's profile and saw they'd posted the same comment on a million billion other videos. They wouldn't have enough time to watch all the stuff they claim to like and run their own gaming channel. More spam, then. But it's okay. I'm sure the real fans will find me soon.

I think I'll take a leaf out of Crafter101's book and post links to my video on other vlogs. Unlike them, I'll actually watch the videos and make genuine comments before including a sneaky link to my own channel.

9PM

My view count is now up to 33. I've had 8 likes and 3 new comments:

Dan_the_legend
POST THIS TO TEN OTHER VIDEOS NOW OR YOU WILL DIE 2NIGHT

Aaron_is_awesome
I AM A SINGER / SONGWRITER CHECK OUT MY CHANNEL I WILL PROVE TO U I AM WORTH IT

Evil Liam 13
Well that's three minutes of my life I won't get back. You suck.

Is it tragic that I'm quite pleased I've been trolled rather than spammed again?

Yes. Yes it is.

10PM

I was just one designer handbag post away from giving up, but a few minutes ago, this came through:

Crazy Kaitlin 2001
Love it! Please make more vids. <3 <3 <3 Destiny.

This was an actual, for-real, positive comment. They weren't trying to sell me sunglasses, they weren't asking me to subscribe to their channel and they weren't even claiming to be a long-lost relative who needed my bank details. They were a genuine fan. RESULT.

WEDNESDAY MARCH 29TH

Over 90 views now. And even more real comments:

 xxFashionGirlxx
OMG more please!

 destinyisperfect
Soooooooooooooooooooooooooooooooooooooooooooooooo oo perfect.

 Jaydenisonfire
Where can I buy that top?

> **Evil Liam 13**
> There's a guy on my street who has Google. I'll ask him.

DatFreakyGrrl
This video was inspirational, thank you SO MUCH for being there.

Planet Kate
Proud of Destiny.

Crazy Kaitlin 2001
Your so awesome

Grammar Leopard
you're

Crazy Kaitlin 2001
Get a life

Chloe C
Room tour next pls

Crazy Kaitlin 2001
Yessss.

Destiny is getting a fandom! This is going to work!

I'm so excited it's ridiculous. I might as well admit it here in my top-secret diary that I haven't made many friends at my new school yet. Or any friends.

It's only been a few weeks, and I know it takes time, but everyone is so stuck in their little groups it's impossible to talk to anyone. It's another reason I decided to actually start a vlog.

I had plenty of friends at my old school — Jess, Sam, Han, Steph when she wasn't being weird. And I still message them. But I feel like I'm fading away now. It takes them longer and longer to reply to my messages every time. Soon they'll be ignoring me altogether.

I thought I'd find a gang like that at my new school, but it hasn't happened yet.

Oh well. I don't care. I'm getting a fandom now. My tactic of posting links on other vlogs must be working. Next, I'll try messaging online stars like Vesper Vlogs on Twitter and see if they'll retweet me. I'll probably end up getting blocked, but it's worth a shot.

In the meantime I need to keep the fans happy, so I'd better do a room tour video next. I'll have to get some new stuff, and also tidy my room tomorrow because the only person who'd want to tour it at the moment would be a pest controller.

Here's how Destiny's room tour should go:

Hi guys, Destiny here, welcome to my room. This is my desk and laptop, where I edit all my videos. This is my dressing table, where I keep all my beauty essentials in immaculate order using home-made desk tidies. This is my bed, where I flop down after a  hard day of vlogging and read your amazing comments. This is my bedside table, where I keep my emergency lip balm ...

And here's how an actual tour of my room would go:

Hi guys, Olivia here, welcome to my room. Here's a pile of dirty laundry on the floor, and next to it here's a pile of clothes I've already worn, but that aren't quite dirty enough for washing just yet. This is the notebook Dad stole from his office and if we lift it up we can see an empty chocolate wrapper and a bag of Cheetos that went out of date in February ...

I think I'd better go for the first option. Which means the fans have managed to make me do something that Mum and Dad never could — actually clean my room.

THURSDAY MARCH 30TH

That was exhausting. It took me all morning to tidy my room, and Dad got really suspicious. He thought I was trying to guilt-trip him into letting me go to New York and he explained over and over again about how we couldn't afford it and no matter how good I was it wouldn't change things.

I didn't want to say I was doing it for a vlog, because then I'd have to explain what a vlog was. He isn't great with technology, which is the understatement of the century. Here's an example. When I was a kid he bought a new monitor for his computer. Before throwing the old one away, he brought it to my room and asked if I'd wipe the files from it so no one could hack into his emails. I couldn't bring myself to tell him it didn't just work like that.

I pretended Emma was coming round to rehearse a play and Mum and Dad seemed pleased. Mum's in a theatre group and she's always wanted me to take an interest, while Dad was just happy I was making new friends.

I wish I were. Emma is only coming round because I'm paying her. She won't even look at me in school, especially when she's with the other Swans.

But things will change if I can go on the trip. I'll get to join the after-school club, which will teach us about the real New York in case we've only ever seen it being protected by superheroes. I can make some proper friends, go on holiday with them at the end of term, and have someone other than Loki and my idiot brother to hang out with this summer.

FRIDAY MARCH 31ST

I woke up to a nice surprise this morning. Vesper Vlogs actually gave me a retweet. That was nice of her, or whoever writes her Twitter.

The new room tour video already has 300 views, 60 likes and plenty of non-spammy comments. Thank you Vesper!

Alyssa S
First

xxFashionGirlxx
I have EXACTLY THE SAME CURTAINS OMG Destiny we are so alike.

Madison Wowowowow
Thumbs up this comment to reveal your secret crush.

DatFreakyGrrl
Destiny > Everyone. FACT

Chloe C
Spring fashion haul video next pls

destinyisperfect
That would be sooooooooooooooooooooooo perfect.

DatFreakyGrrl
Yes. That.

Jaydenisonfire
At last we have a video where ALL the comments are respectful and polite.

Evil Liam 13
Your mother is respectful and polite.

I'm so excited, I love it that fans are suggesting new videos. I just wish they wouldn't suggest such expensive ones. If I went on a spring shopping haul it would wipe out the rest of my savings. Hmm.

7PM

I've got it. I'll blow my savings on new clothes tomorrow, but I'll keep the receipts and take them back the day after. The fans get the video they want, and I get my precious savings back. Boom.

SATURDAY APRIL 1ST

SPRING HAUL | THE DESTINY CHANNEL

Hey guys, welcome to my spring haul. Sorry, I went a bit crazy out there today because ... well, of course I did. The first thing I bought was this thin jumper, which I'm absolutely loving right now. It's so hard for me to find tops that look right on my shoulders 'cos they're sooo freakishly wide.

[It wasn't the first thing I bought. It was the fourth thing, after a Mars, some Doritos and a can of Fanta. I'd spent all morning leafing through fashion magazines and needed to get my strength up before putting my new style expertise into practice.]

Let me just hold that up for you … Check it out! A row of sequins around the collar. That's so Destiny, right?

Next I got this cute shirt, which has these amazing little pops of yellow. How spring is that? I just know I'm going to keep it forever.

[I'm not. It's currently in my closet with all the rest of the stuff, wrapped in five plastic bags so Loki can't mistake it for his litter tray and make it impossible to return.]

At first Emma didn't want to say the bit about Destiny's shoulders being freakishly wide, but I explained it was part of the character. All the best vloggers pretend they're hideous, even if they're actually gorgeous. That's just what you have to do these days. You can't brag, you have to humblebrag.

Instead of saying, 'I've just been announced as the new face of L'Oreal,' you have to say, 'Wow, I can't believe I'm the new face of L'Oreal. Haven't they seen my massive bum chin?' And instead of saying, 'I've just been invited to Kanye West's birthday party,' you have to say, 'I can't believe I'm going to be rubbing shoulders with all those celebs. What could a nobody like me possibly have to say to them?'

Emma went along with it, but she seemed kind of annoyed. She's always a bit grumpy when she comes round, like she's worried she'll catch loser disease from me. But as soon as I say we're recording she comes across as the sort of best friend I wish I had.

She even stayed in character to do a live stream where she read out the best comments on the video.

I thought this would be a good way to build up a loyal fanbase, but we had to abandon it after a few minutes because my brother Charlie kept running around outside my room, making high-pitched noises and giggling.

In the end I got rid of him by threatening to show Mum and Dad the doorbell video. He got his friend Michael to film him ringing all the doorbells on our street last week. I pretended I found it really funny and asked him to send it to me. Obviously I just wanted it to blackmail him with, but he was too stupid to work it out.

SUNDAY APRIL 2ND

Taking all the clothes back was really awkward. I said they were the wrong size, which was true, but the customer service staff must have wondered what kind of deluded idiot buys an entire wardrobe three sizes too small.

Every time I checked my phone I saw a new comment, and that cheered me up between all the shame:

Crazy Kaitlin 2001
How spring is that <3 <3 <3

xxFashionGirlxx
OMG I bought that exact same top this week we are so alike.

CourtenyOMG
Dstiny in best I allways watch UR video LOL
Translate

Pedantic Penguin
Your English is so bad I've just been given the option to translate it.

CourtenyOMG
If U dont lik it dont red LOL
Translate

destinyisperfect
Your shoulders are not *freakishly wide* They are perfect.

Poppy M
This video is soooo amazing

SHOUTING LAUREN
DESTINY!!!!!!!!!!!!!!!!!!!!!!!!!!! WOOOOO

Koharu99
I am from Tokyo

 DestinyMonster02
Love U Destiny.

The video got to 500 views by lunchtime, but since then it's only crept up to 700. That's a solid fanbase, but it's not going to get me to New York.

I've checked the option on my account that means I'll get a share of the profits if my fans click on the adverts. It's impossible to work out how many viewers I'd need, but basically it's a lot more.

In other words, Destiny needs to go viral.

Okay. Maybe I should involve Loki. Cat videos always go viral. I could get him to pull a funny face like Grumpy Cat, or strike a funny pose like Surprised Kitten, or creep around in a funny way like Ninja Cat. He's bound to do something hilarious if I promise him a biscuit. And if he ever wakes up.

8PM

Well that didn't work. I filmed Loki for over an hour and he did nothing but sleep on the radiator. The only way I can guarantee to get him moving would be to put the vacuum on. But that would just make him hide under the bed, which is hardly viral gold.

Okay, I need a better idea.

I've got it! I'll give Destiny a boyfriend. Vlogging

couples are always crazily popular. I'll have to pay for another actor, which will double the cost of each recording. But if I can make them adorable enough, the fans will spread the word and the channel will get hundreds of thousands of views, rather than just hundreds. That's surely got to be enough to get me the fanbase I need.

MONDAY APRIL 3RD

INTRODUCING GALE | THE DESTINY CHANNEL

Welcome to all my new subscribers. I love you guys SO MUCH! This time I'm going to introduce you to someone really special. No, it's not Loki again, it's my amazing boyfriend Gale. Ta-dah!

[I got a guy from Emma's theatre group who could play 'Gale' at short notice. He's actually called Callum and he seems pretty dumb. He kept asking what his motivation was. I already promised to pay him £10. What more does he want? But he's hot and the fans will fall for him, I'm sure.]

Give the fans a wave, Gale! Isn't he awesome?

[I wanted to call Destiny's boyfriend Jacob, or Michael or Josh, or something else from the list of most popular boy's names, but Emma insisted on calling him Gale because of *The Hunger Games*. It's not even a boys' name. We might as well call him Katniss.]

Today we're going to play the whisper challenge. Here's how it goes. Gale wears these headphones and I whisper things to him. He has to work out what I'm saying by reading my lips. Then we swap, and whoever gets the fewest points has to make the other's favourite meal.

I wouldn't say Callum is the best actor in the world. I wouldn't even say he was the best actor in the room — Loki totally convinced me yesterday that he hadn't already been fed. But if I stick to challenge videos it should make things easier for him. All he has to do is focus on winning the game and forget about acting and it will come across as natural.

I wrote a good ending for this video, even if I say so

myself. Gale wins the challenge, meaning Destiny has to do the cooking. But then he reveals he's done it anyway, and goes downstairs to fetch Destiny's favourite meal of pepperoni pizza. They hug and share a slice. The video ends. The fans love it. I get to go to New York. Hopefully.

After the recording was over I got Emma and Callum to come up with ideas about their characters, because I thought it might help with future videos. Turns out I thought wrong.

Emma came up with a complicated backstory about how Destiny had been mute until the age of eight, when seeing her first ever online video inspired her to start talking, and ever since then she'd dedicated her life to becoming the greatest ever vlogger.

Callum came up with an even less likely one about how they'd fallen in love in an airport, missed their flights and the planes had collided in mid-air, killing everyone on board.

I jotted down their ideas and promised to use them

in the future. When they'd gone I tore the page out of my notebook and threw it away. So much for getting the acting talent to help out.

10PM

I posted the video two hours ago and I've had 316 views, 186 likes and 12 comments already:

Chloe C
Love U both

Planet Kate
Gale 4ever

xxFashionGirlxx
2:04 Oh my god …

Flames R Us
I HOPE U BOTH DIE

IPAD BARGAINZ
RETAILERS HATE THIS LOOPHOLE! BRAND NEW IPADS
FOR UNDER $30!

>
> **Chloe C**
> How do you eat pizza and stay thin?
>
> **Crazy Kaitlin 2001**
> Gale <3 <3 <3

TUESDAY APRIL 4TH

The Gale video was up to over 1000 views when I checked it this morning! The comment with the most likes was:

> **Leah Yeah Yeah**
> Thumbs up if you came here from Clickfeed.

I went to the Clickfeed site and between '14 Cats Having a Way Worse Day Than You' and '18 Things You'll Only Understand if You Have Strict Parents' was a listicle called 'Ten New Vlogs You Need to Watch Right Now'. The Destiny Channel was number eight on the list.

Most of the others vlogs had been recently retweeted by Vesper Vlogs too, so they probably didn't spend too long researching it. But I'm not complaining.

Every time I checked I had more views. I looked at my phone so much in class that Mr Robinson confiscated it until after school. When I finally got it back I thought there must have been a mistake. The view count had gone up to 15,000.

By the time I was home, the view count had gone up to 20,000. It's 10pm now and it's just gone past 30,000.

This is it. I'm going viral.

Okay, okay, I need to keep calm. Must sleep, mustn't think about views, must sleep, mustn't think about views.

1AM

45,000 views now. Yay!

WEDNESDAY APRIL 5TH

Over 60,000 now. I tried to tell Emma at lunchtime, but she was sitting with the Swans and she totally blanked me.

The Swans is obviously a stupid name, and they're only called that because the ringleader, Jasmine, is meant to look like Bella Swan from *Twilight*. Except she doesn't really look like her, she just bites her lower lip all the time like that actress did. I think the name was supposed to mock them, but they took it as a compliment.

The only other Swan apart from Emma and Jasmine is Grace. A girl called Chloe used to be in the gang too, but they threw her out for wearing school shoes on no-uniform day. That's how harsh they are.

To be fair to Emma, she did tell me not to act like her friend if I saw her in school. She said it the first time she came round. But she seems so friendly when she's playing Destiny I forget what she's really like.

At lunchtime I sat down opposite her and said 'hi'. She looked away, as did the other Swans. I felt like telling the silent lip-biters to get over themselves, but I just stared down at the table and ate my Doritos.

So guess what? I'm going to keep all the good news about the vlog to myself. If Emma's going to be like that she doesn't deserve to know we're going viral, and she doesn't deserve a slice of the profits when they roll in. She can stick to her £10 fee while I make millions.

If she complains I'll just look the other way and pretend I can't hear her, in proper Swan style.

8PM

I was reading through all the comments on the Gale video this evening when I saw this one:

> **?** Jack C
> Fake

I was so shocked I spat Fanta over my keyboard, which at least meant I had to clean it for once. Was this guy on to us? Everyone else seemed convinced by Emma and Callum, so how had he seen through them?

I clicked through to Jack C's profile and it showed his recent activity.

RECENT ACTIVITY

> **?** **Jack C** commented on the video <u>Crazy Student Sets Fire to School Canteen</u>.
> Fake

Jack C commented on the video <u>Guy Loses an Arm in Shark Attack</u>.
Fake. Look at 0:55 his arm is clearly made of rubber, it's so bendy. This is staged.

Jack C commented on the video <u>Woman Crashes Through Convenience Store Window</u>.
Fake

Jack C commented on the video <u>Woman Loses it in Wendys</u>.
Fake. This is an actress.

Jack C commented on the video <u>1969 Moon Landings</u>.
Fake. 2:33 There is no air on the moon so the flag should not be waving. This was filmed in a movie studio.

It was okay. Jack C was one of those people who insist everything they ever see is fake. None of my fans bothered arguing with him and his comment was soon washed away on a tide of Gale and Destiny fan love.

Crisis over. Phew.

THURSDAY APRIL 6TH

The last video has had over 80,000 views now. That's enough to fill a stadium. Maybe I should hire one and get Emma and Callum to play the whisper game live.

Even though I took my dinner up to my room and ate it while I was reading the comments, Mum made me come down and load the dishwasher. It didn't seem right that someone with 80,000 fans should still have to do chores. Surely I should have an entourage to take care of that sort of thing now.

Online success is a weird thing. You can be broadcasting to tens of thousands of fans one minute and the next you're scraping soggy broccoli into a bin. And they wonder why I hate leaving my bedroom.

FRIDAY APRIL 7TH

Destiny was sent a message from someone called 'Sparkle Smiles' this morning:

Hi Destiny! We love your vlog and think you'd be a great fit for our brand. DM us your postal address if you're interested in an exciting promotion deal.

I had no idea what Sparkle Smiles were, or what they were asking me to do, but I spotted the words 'promotion' and 'deal' and thought it might involve money, so I told them I was interested.

SATURDAY APRIL 8TH

I was woken up by the doorbell early this morning. A minute later Dad brought a huge 'Sparkle Smiles' box to my room. He lectured me about spending money on things I didn't need as I tried to rip the box open.

When I finally got inside I found a load of bubble wrap and eight white packets containing tiny golden stars, hearts and dolphins. They looked like earrings, but didn't seem to have any attachments.

At the bottom of the box was a tiny pot of glue and a letter.

Dear Destiny,

We're so pleased you've accepted our offer. As agreed, we enclose your complimentary Sparkle Smiles tooth jewels. It would be great if you could wear them while recording your next vlog and draw attention to them in a way that feels natural. You could lift your lip up and say, 'These Sparkle Smiles tooth jewels are so on trend. If I were you I'd go to sparklesmiles.com and buy some right now. That address again is sparklesmiles.com.'

Feel free to return the unopened boxes to us if you don't think this will work for your brand.

Thanks so much for agreeing to this and I hope you're as excited as we are.

Felicity Hamilton-Johnson
Social Marketing Manager
Sparkle Smiles

I'm not really sure what to do. I was hoping to be paid in money rather than tacky jewellery. On the other hand, I'm quite pleased the vlog has already caught the attention of someone with the job title 'Social Marketing Manager'. And I'm amazed to discover the videos we made in my bedroom are a 'brand'.

I've already opened the boxes so I can't really return them. On the other hand, the tooth jewels are really awful. I tried wearing them but they kept falling off, and they made my mouth taste of envelopes.

Maybe I could make some money by selling them in school. But everyone already thinks I'm weird. I'd be an outcast forever if I tried to flog dodgy jewels that make you look like the world's cheapest gangsta rapper. Why did I ever agree to this?

SUNDAY APRIL 9TH

Okay. I'm going to play hardball. I started this vlog to make enough for the New York trip, not to fill my mouth with what look like stray fillings. I've researched marketing lingo online and written an email demanding payment, sent from a Destiny email account I had to create.

Sparkle Smiles and Destiny Vlog
From: Destiny
Sunday, 9 April 19:32
To: Felicity Hamilton-Johnson

Dear Felicity Hamilton-Johnson,

Thank you so much for the boxes of Sparkle Smiles tooth jewellery. As you will be aware, my vlog has a regular audience of over 100,000. As such, it is a unique promotional opportunity to reach a key demographic.

Because of this, I use standard rates for product placement. The rate for me to mention your tooth jewels will be £100. I'm afraid this is non-negotiable. However, as my channel reaches high-end ABC1 consumers, I'm sure you'll agree this cost is fair.

If this is acceptable please send the funds to the bank account linked to my secretary's email address: oliviajdwarren@gmail.com

Kind regards
Destiny

MONDAY APRIL 10TH

The reply came through to my phone during history this afternoon.

Re: Sparkle Smiles and Destiny Vlog
From: Felicity Hamilton-Johnson
Monday, 10 April 14:02
To: Destiny

No problem. Sending funds through now,

F

And that was it. I checked my bank account and the money was there. I was so shocked I couldn't concentrate on my worksheet.

Is it that easy to make money? All my life I've begged for more allowance, yet this Felicity woman pops up from nowhere and gives me free money.

I wondered if I should have held out for more. Felicity agreed to £100 straight away. What if I'd asked for double that? Triple? More? How much do these people have to throw around? Felicity could spend £500 every day on mineral water and croissants for all I know. I'll just have to drive a harder bargain next time I'm offered something like this.

In the meantime, I need to keep my part of the deal. Time to write a script with some subtle product placement.

TUESDAY APRIL 11TH

APRIL FAVOURITES | THE DESTINY CHANNEL

Hey guys. Just thought I'd have a quick chat about what I'm loving at the moment. First up I'm super super loving this medium brown sculpting brow mascara. Let me show you it in action ... Check. That. Out.

[Emma had a metal star, half moon and dolphin stuck to her teeth as she did the mascara demo.

We had to do four takes because they kept spinning off on to my keyboard. One of the love hearts got stuck next to the 'v' key and I was on the verge of renaming the video 'April Stuff I Like' before I finally managed to dislodge it.]

The next thing I'm loving this month are these Sparkle Smiles tooth jewels. Trust me, these are going to take off in a big big way. You'll find them on their website sparklesmiles.com. They come with their own glue that won't permanently damage your teeth. Look how they reflect the light – so pretty. Want!

[At this point I got Emma to lift up her lip and show the jewels to the camera. They all sprang out again, but I managed to cut to the next April favourite just before they did.]

I've uploaded the video now and I think I got away with it. The tooth jewels were just one of five April favourites, and the others were all good-quality things. I should only feel 20% guilty.

The problem was that Emma got so annoyed by the taste of glue she didn't get into the role as much as usual. Her performance was quite flat and she kept saying she wanted to go home whenever I asked for another take.

She also stormed off after we'd finished, so we couldn't do the live stream thing where she reads out the comments as they come in. But I think that might have been because I offered to pay her in tooth jewels instead of cash. It was worth a try.

10PM

So far the video has had 1752 views and just 143 likes, which is well below the usual level. I've even had 37 thumbs down, and I usually get

fewer than 10. The comments were much more mixed too:

X Katy X
Meh

Leah Yeah Yeah
I love all your videos, keep them coming. Destiny fandom 4 ever.

Chloe C
Those teeth jewel things look gross.

Evil Liam 13
You look like you were chewing gold spinach and got some stuck in your teeth.

ThatztottalyCate
Thnaks for thes vidz.

Ant The Pedant
Well done. You managed to spell three out of the four words in your comment wrong.

ThatztottalyCate
Haterz gon hat

OMG AMY
0:15 Would this work also with supercurler black mascara?

Finn Funn
Do not under any circumstances attempt this with supercurler black mascara. Your life and the lives of your family would be in danger.

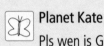
Planet Kate
Pls wen is Gale coming back?

WEDNESDAY APRIL 12TH

I'm starting to feel guilty about the tooth jewels now. I really hope none of the fans bought them.

I can't think about it now, anyway. I've got to write the script for tomorrow's video.

I need to make Destiny and Gale as adorable as I can, so the fans will be even more upset when I break them up in a couple of weeks.

Oh, did I mention I'm going to split the golden couple

up soon? It will get the fans talking, more people will find out about the vlog, and the view counts will shoot up. Mwah ha ha.

THURSDAY APRIL 13TH

HOW WELL DO WE KNOW EACH OTHER? | THE DESTINY CHANNEL

Hey guys! You asked for him and here he is. The one and only Gale is back! Ta-dah!

[At this point Callum was meant to jump in and land on the chair next to Emma, but he overbalanced and ended up on the floor. Emma managed to stay in character and shouted, 'Oh my god, Gale, I am so keeping that in!']

Today we're doing a challenge called 'How Well Do We Know Each Other?' It's really, really simple. I'll ask Gale questions about me, he'll ask me questions about him, whoever gets the most wrong has to buy the other a present. Try it at home with your boyfriends, girlfriends, sisters, brothers, best friends, whoever.

Emma and Callum kept collapsing into hysterics after the chair thing. I had to edit the final video from five different takes.

In my original script, they were both meant to get all the questions right until the very end, when Gale gets Destiny's favourite colour wrong and says green instead of the real answer, purple. She gets upset, but then he gives her a purple teddy hugging a love heart to prove he knew the answer all along.

The problem was they were laughing so much they didn't even get halfway through the script. I was pretty annoyed while we were filming — I'd spent time honing that script to perfection. But when I edited the video together I had to admit it worked well. Better than if they'd stuck to my version, maybe.

I guess that's something to keep in mind. People watch vlogs because they want them to feel real. If they wanted fake they could watch blockbuster movies where bald men walk away from exploding cars in slow motion. If Emma and Callum improvise and it feels natural, I should use it in the video, whatever I had planned.

This video shot up to over 5000 views right away, and the fans much preferred it to the tooth jewel one:

Pixie Sunshine YAY
All the feels.

Poppy M
OMG I can't even …

Aleksandra Love Heart
0:15 LMAO

Kanye West Is Your Mother
I'm going to be sick.

Pixie Sunshine YAY
We don't care about your childish comments, we just ignore them.

Kanye West Is Your Mother
I see. You don't care. That's why you bothered to reply.

Chloe C

Cutest couple on the internet #Gestiny

 SHOUTING LAUREN

OMG HES LIKE SO CUTE WHEN HE COMES ON IM LIKE
IM SCREAMING AND MOM WAS LIKE WHAT WAS THAT
BUT IM LIKE HES HOT SO WHATEVER LOL

 Leah Yeah Yeah

I never want you to break up ever.

 DatFreakyGrrl

Don't even oh my god …

 Pixie Sunshine YAY

I would be destroyed.

 Abi To The Gail

Four dislikes??? Who would even dislike this???

Evil Liam 13

Me.

10PM

All my old friends from school have stopped texting me back now. I've had no replies to the last messages I sent to Jess, Sam, Han and Steph. I'm not surprised about Steph, and I wasn't even sure about keeping in touch with her anyway, but I thought the others would at least send me a smiley. We're talking about two taps of a screen. Surely that's not too much to ask.

I'm going to have to move on now or I'll start looking desperate. Bye, old school friends.

In the meantime I've got all the comments from the Destiny fans to read. I've never met these people, and most don't even live in this country, but at least they're bothering to write to me. Or to Destiny. Whatever.

FRIDAY APRIL 14TH

The day after I write about needing to make friends, someone new sits next to me in chemistry.

But here's the bad news. It's not someone I would ever EVER want to hang around with.

I always sit on the desk at the front because it's the only one that's free. The Swans sit at the back, everyone else sits in the middle and I have to go at the front like I'm such a big chemistry fan that I want the best view possible.

I've got so used to sitting alone I always put my bag on the other seat. But today a boy called Sebastian asked if the seat was free. As I was moving my rucksack to the floor, his breath hit me and I wished I'd refused.

He smelled like cheesy puffs, and my suspicions were confirmed when he started speaking and I could see bright orange crumbs stuck between his braces and teeth.

And the things he said were just as annoying as the smell. He was one of those people who feel the need to boast about absolutely everything.

He told me about how he'd scored a perfect game last time he went bowling, how he got the highest mark in three years on the maths test and how he's so naturally good with computers that they banned him from the lunchtime coding club. Yeah, I'm sure his breath had nothing to do with it.

I stared down at my worksheet and blocked him out, but he still wouldn't take the hint. He went on and on about how he'd completed the new *Call of Duty* game on expert setting. I told him I wasn't really into games (Translation: shut up shut up shut up), but he kept going.

I didn't want to be mean to
Sebastian, but if I encouraged him
he'd sit next to me every lesson and
then at lunchtimes too and then
everyone would start thinking I
smelled of cheesy puffs too and we'd become the
cheesy puff gang and my life would be over. I know
it's harsh, but that's how school works.

6PM

My brother barged in this evening and announced
he'd been listening at the door and he knows I've
invented a fake vlogger. He threatened to tell
Mum and Dad that I'd been lying to people, so I
said I'll tell them about the time he blocked the
sinks in the shopping centre with paper towels. I'm
glad he boasts about all the stupid stuff he
does. It means I'm never short of stuff to blackmail
him with.

10PM

Thanks to my stupid brother I've spent the whole

evening worrying about whether I'm misleading the Destiny fans. The vlog's taken off so fast I haven't thought about it much.

Okay. Here's where I've got to.

Most people put across a fake version of themselves online. Like they'll post on Facebook and Instagram when they're heading out to a party, but not when they're staying in to watch sad films on Netflix and use their cat as a hanky. And a lot of celebrities get their minions to write their tweets, their songs, their books and everything else, and this isn't so different.

As long as the fans enjoy the vlog, it doesn't matter if it's real or not. Worry over.

SATURDAY APRIL 15TH

I didn't want Charlie's threat hanging over me, so I decided to confess everything to Mum and Dad myself.

I told them that I hadn't really been rehearsing for a play with Emma and Callum, but recording a vlog. I told them we'd created a character called Destiny, and some of our fans thought she was real, but it wasn't serious because lots of online stuff that's meant to be real is actually fake.

I thought they were going to lecture me on dishonesty, but they were actually fine with it. Neither of them knew what a vlog was, and I think they imagined it was a kind of short film. Mum's forced us to sit through lots of terrible plays and musicals by her amateur theatre group over the years, but for once there was an upside to her hobby. She was really impressed that I'd written some 'vlog films' and chosen the cast all on my own. She's even offered to bring drinks and snacks up when Emma and Callum come round again tomorrow.

To make things even better, they got angry with Charlie when I told them how he'd tried to interrupt us. Ha.

SUNDAY APRIL 16TH

I should have known not to accept Mum's offer of drinks and snacks. She deliberately waited until we were running through the script, then burst in. Before she'd even offered them anything she started describing some of the warm-up exercises she does with her acting group and asked Emma and Callum to try them. They were too confused to do anything but what they were told, so for the next ten minutes she had them scrunching into balls, pretending to be flowers and falling backwards into each other's arms.

It was absolutely no use whatsoever, and only used up valuable time when we could have been filming.

When I'd got rid of Mum, we were finally able to make the new video. Emma and Callum were brilliant first time, which is just as well, because they'd have been too exhausted from all the flower impersonations to do retakes.

GALE DOES MY MAKEUP | THE DESTINY CHANNEL

Hey guys! Don't panic, there's nothing wrong with your screens. I'm just not wearing my makeup today. Scary naked face! And that's because Gale is going to do it for me. ARGH! What have I let myself in for?

[It was tough to persuade Emma to remove her makeup for this. I told her all serious actors have to transform themselves for big roles and if she ever wants to win an Oscar she'll have to make herself look like something that needs Horcruxes to survive.]

Gale: I have literally never even picked up eyeliner before. This is insane.

Destiny: Okay, give me a winged line. You have no idea what I'm talking about, do you?

Gale: Don't diss my makeup skills. Wait till I've finished, then diss them.

I wrote a whole script for Emma and Callum, but they soon started improvising. I remembered my lesson from the last video, and left them to it. Callum tried to draw flowery swirls underneath Emma's eyes, but he messed up and turned them into black splodges that made her look like an emo panda.

By the end of the video, Callum and Emma had smeared so much lipstick over their faces they looked like scary clowns. They went from adorable couple to something you'd dream up after eating too much cheese.

The video got 547 likes in the first hour, more than the tooth jewel video has got the whole time it's been up. And the comments were very positive:

 Leah Yeah Yeah
U R beautiful your face isn't scary without makeup oh god don't even say that

 destinyisperfect
Destiny is perfect even without her makeup.

 Aleksandra Love Heart
Destiny and Gale <3 <3 <3

Isabella365
I would totally let Gale do my makeup

 OMG AMY
LOL Same

Finn Funn
You looked so weird after Gale had done your makeup.
And before.

 Poppy M
Ba Dum Tsh.

 xxFashionGirlxx
#LMAO #ROFL #NOTREALLY

 SHOUTING LAUREN
I'M WATCHING THIS AND IM LIKE ACTUALLY CRYING AND
EVERYONE IS LIKE SHUT UP AND IM LIKE I DON'T CARE

 Priya Hearts Vlogs
I ship Destiny and Gale

 Grammar Leopard
What? Is that even English?

 Priya Hearts Vlogs
Yeah its short for relationship everyone knows
that except you LOL.

 Finn Funn
I would ship them to Antarctica.

MONDAY APRIL 17TH

Dad came into my room tonight and asked me how the vlogging was going. I was so shocked he'd even remembered the right word I couldn't speak. Then he asked me how many web hits I'd had and whether I'd put it on iPads yet, and I worked out what was going on.

Every now and then an article about modern stuff turns up in his newspaper and he reads it to take an interest in my hobbies. It's sort of sweet but also a little bit (a lot) embarrassing.

Dad managed to say plenty of the right words, even if they weren't quite in the right order. He did a lot better than I'd have done if I'd tried to talk about his football team, for instance. But the cringing made my cheeks so hot I had to go to the bathroom and splash cold water on them when he'd finished. Well done, Dad. Thanks for taking an interest. But I won't be upset if you give the tech guru routine a rest in future.

TUESDAY APRIL 18TH

Another product placement offer came through to Destiny's channel this morning. This one was for something called 'Poxytolin Slimming Cream'. I Googled it and every review said it was useless. One woman said it gave her a rash and another said it made her smell like a bathroom floor. There's no way I could push that on the fans. Who'd want to put something like that on themselves?

I got back to Poxytolin straight away and said it wasn't right for my brand. I could have said more about how they shouldn't be marketing this to teenagers but I was trying to be professional. This was their reply:

That's a shame as we are willing to offer £500 for a positive review. Please send us your home address and payment details if you change your mind.

Now I don't know what to do.

£500 is a lot of money. That would cover my flight to New York. All I have to do is sneak a good review of the slimming cream into the next video.

I started the vlog so I could go to New York. If I take the slimming cream deal, I'll have done that already. I can delete the Destiny account and get on with my life. But first I'd have to trick the fans into buying a cream that burns their skin and makes them smell of floor.

And could I really live with myself after flogging rip-off slimming products? I'm not exactly stick thin and I don't care. I don't want to promote something that exploits people who worry about their size.

But £500 is a lot. DILEMMA.

WEDNESDAY APRIL 19TH

This is not good.

My first ad revenue payment, for when viewers click through the adverts that appear on my site, came through today and it was just £27.56.

I know the vlog hasn't been going that long, but I was really hoping for more.

It would take me years to save up for the New York trip at this rate. I'm really thinking I should just take the diet cream money and forget about it.

THURSDAY APRIL 20TH

I was on the verge of accepting the diet cream cash this evening. But just before I did, I checked back on the tooth jewel video. It had been given 406 more dislikes and only 15 more likes. And there were lots of worrying new comments:

xxFashionGirlxx
OMG we are so alike. I'm ordering Sparkle Smiles right now!

Crazy Kaitlin 2001
I bought a pack of these tooth jewels after watching this video. One of them fell off while I was eating and cracked my filling. Why did you say they were good?

Chloe C
I wore the tooth jewels to school this morning and everyone teased me and said I was trying to look cool. Then I got sent home for breaking school uniform rules because I couldn't take them off. I've got an appointment with the dentist tomorrow to have them removed.

Jaydenisonfire
My tooth jewels arrived yesterday. I had to use so much glue to keep them on it upset my stomach and I had an accident in class. NO ONE SHOULD EVER BUY THEM.

Reading these comments made me feel awful. These were the same fans who'd got behind the vlog from the start and how had I repaid them? I'd tricked them into buying useless rubbish that sent them fleeing to the nearest dentist or toilet.

I couldn't bring myself to tell them to buy the slimming cream too. I just couldn't.

I forced myself to reply to the cream people and tell them I still didn't think they were right for my brand. I felt like New York was getting further away with every letter I typed. But I'm glad I did it.

FRIDAY APRIL 21ST

I'm not going to take any more money for dodgy product placement. I'm going to earn enough for the New York trip, and I'm going to do it through ad money alone. That means I've got to make videos that will get hundreds of thousands of views, not just thousands.

I can't wait any longer to split up Gale and Destiny. I'm going to do it in the next video.

SATURDAY APRIL 22ND

MORNING EYE-MAKEUP ROUTINE | THE DESTINY CHANNEL

Hey guys. Today I'll be taking you through my morning eye-makeup routine. Which means we're going to begin with my scary naked face again. Sorry not sorry!

I start off with a light concealer, dabbing it under my eyes. I usually blend it with a large brush like this. Be careful not to get it in your eyes, especially if you've just woken up. We all know what it's like. You pressed the snooze button too many times, you have to do your makeup in the three minutes before the bus arrives, disaster looms.

[I had to ask Emma about her morning eye-makeup routine to write this, as I don't have one. I have a bad relationship with makeup. Whenever I put it on I feel like everyone's staring at me.]

Next comes the eye shadow. I'm taking a stiff domed brush along the crease of my eye and blending it outwards. Let me lean in so you can see.

Then I put on my eyeliner, using a standard eye pencil ...

Whoops, that's my phone. I'll just reject the call ...

Er ... okay guys, it's Gale. I need to take this. Back in a minute.

[At this point Emma made herself cry using a method she'd learned in drama school where you have to think of something really sad. I'd think about all the money I lost from turning down the diet cream promotion.]

I'm sorry. I can't go on right now. Gale just called me and ... I don't even know how to say this ...

He wants to break up.

I'm sorry. You'll have to give me a minute.

[I cut again while Emma made herself cry some more. It didn't help that we could hear Charlie laughing from his room. His laugh is really annoying, like a seal being run over. But Emma managed to work herself up until the mascara was running down her cheeks and it looked really dramatic.]

He said he needed some space and that it wasn't me, it was him. He said he wasn't in the right place for commitment.

I'm going to leave it here, guys. But keep your comments coming. They mean so much to me.

It turned out Emma had got herself so much into the character she still felt sad even after we finished filming. I had to fetch a box of tissues and tell her how brilliant she was for half an hour. Eventually she cheered up and thanked me for writing such a good script. You'd never guess she was the same person who blanks me in the lunch hall.

I uploaded the video this evening and went down for dinner. Mum and Dad have this weird rule that I'm not allowed to look at my phone during mealtimes so we can all sit together and talk as a family. The main thing I talk about is how I wish I could look at my phone.

Today was even worse than usual. How many likes and comments was I missing as I shovelled in Dad's chicken pasta? I ate it so quickly I actually gave myself hiccups. Soon everyone will have Wi-Fi in their brains so their parents can't cut them off from the world just for the sake of family mealtimes.

By the time it was over the new video already had over 5000 views and 400 likes. It had 200 dislikes too, but I'm sure they meant they disliked Destiny getting dumped rather than the video itself.

I began to feel a little guilty as the comments poured in, because some of the fans were really upset. But I told myself they were upset in a good way, like when you cry at the end of a slushy film.

xxFashionGirlxx
OMG

 DestinyMonster02
ZOMG

 Leah Yeah Yeah
XOMG

 Abi To The Gail
Unable

 DatFreakyGrrl
So sorry to hear this, Destiny. You still have us and we will always be there for you. If there is anything we can do let us know.

 Sweet Kitten Buttercup
GALE YOU WILL TAKE DESTINY BACK. IF YOU DO NOT I WILL LOOK FOR YOU AND I WILL BREAK YOU.

 Poppy M
When you're trying to hold back the tears but life is too much.

Planet Kate
He did not deserve you. #proudofdestiny

Crazy Kaitlin 2001
I am happy because now you will have more time for us.

 Chloe C
If you were a true fan you would want her to be happy for herself.

 Evil Liam 13
It's probably because he saw you without makeup on.

 Queen Ashley III
Pls make another video let us know your alright.

 Pixie Sunshine YAY
This hit me in the feels.

 Kanya2003
Destiny I am sending my love and support from Chiang Mai in northern Thailand.

 Lothario99
I'm a single guy and I think we should get together now you are single too. Message me for coffee.

 Queen Ashley III
OMG literally she has just broken up. Men are dogs.

SUNDAY APRIL 23RD

The Gale and Destiny breakup video already has over 50,000 views. And I've been sent a new message:

Hi Destiny

So sorry to hear about your relationship troubles. I've been there myself and let me tell you it DOES get better.

In the meantime I'd like to offer you an exciting opportunity to get on board with GlamValue, one of the most talked-about budget cosmetics brands in the world.

Here's the deal:

We send you a box of our non-run mascara and you include it in your next tutorial. Halfway through, you break down and reminisce about Gale. For example, you could remember a time when you walked along a beach at sunset. That's just a starting point – run with it and have fun.

As you cry again, you point out that your mascara isn't running. We think this would be a fab real-life product demo.

We will offer you a one-off fee of £500 for this.

Let me know what you think,

Karen Spicer
Social Imagineer
GlamValue Cosmetics

Again, I'm very tempted. If Karen Spicer is starting at £500, maybe I can get her up to £1000. Also, most of the online reviews say the mascara is actually pretty good, so I won't be tricking any fans this time.

Hmm ...

MONDAY APRIL 24TH

No. I promised myself I wouldn't take any more product placements. And this Karen 'imagineer' woman seems really insensitive. If Destiny were real, imagine how upset she'd be at someone trying to cash in on her misery.

Oh well. At least I got to write a message that made me feel good:

Dear Karen Spicer

I'm afraid I cannot accept your offer to demonstrate your non-run mascara with my tears. This is a difficult time for me and I have more important things to think about. Also, MY FEELINGS ARE NOT FOR SALE.

Destiny

TUESDAY APRIL 25TH

SPRING SALE HAUL | THE DESTINY CHANNEL

Hi guys. So sorry about last time. But it's all behind me now and we're back to business as usual.

Normal service has
been resumed! And
guess what? It's haul
time. I've been trawling
the sales for bargains ...
Yay! We love bargains!

First up is this pink jumper. I picked this up for just
a few pounds, can you believe it? It's very soft and
super super pretty. But be warned, it's a bit see-
through. Well, a lot see-through. Look at my hand
underneath it. So wear it on top of something else
or ... error!

Next up is this blue vest top. This was just ... I got
this ...

[At this point Emma made herself think about sad
things again. She tried to smile, but her bottom lip
wobbled and tears rolled down her cheeks. It was
really convincing. I wish I could make myself
distraught on cue like that. I'd have to watch a
whole box set of weepy movies while chopping onions to
get myself in that state.]

Sorry guys. This has been more difficult for me than I expected. I'm not in a great place, and I think maybe I should give the vlog a rest. But thanks so much for your comments. You're such a big part of my life and I care just as much about you as you do about me. But maybe I need to take a break ...

[At this point Emma buried her face in the pink jumper and sobbed, which was a good bit of improvisation, but I don't think I can take it back now. You can't return cried-in clothes, even if you keep the receipt. Now I wish I'd at least asked for a free sample of the non-run mascara.]

The view count for this video shot past 50,000 almost instantly. The fans are obviously desperate for the next episodes in the saga, even if they only feature Destiny snivelling into a bargain.

The comments flooded in once again:

Floral Print Flora
OMG I can't believe what has happen. This is awful.

 Its Me Sophie
Sending hugs

 Koharu99
I am visiting from Tokyo next month and would like to
stay in your house. What is your house address?

 Thats so Katy
Don't worry. Everything happens for a reason.

     Evil Liam 13
    And sometimes the reason is that you're really
    annoying.

 Poppy M
wipes tears away I will never forgive Gale for what he
has done to us.

 PlanetLover382
Guys, let's get some perspective here. Why are we all
getting worked up about this when there are issues such
as the destruction of the rainforests in South America?

xxFashionGirlxx
That is not what this video is about. OMG shut up. People like you make me so angry.

PlanetLover382
I'm sorry if I made you angry. My aim was merely to get us to think about wider issues.

Sabrina Pony Lover
We will always love you whatever that SNAKE Gale does.

WEDNESDAY APRIL 26TH

I woke up early this morning and couldn't get back to sleep, so I went online and watched the views and comments rack up. It was great to know that even then, as the first streaks of pink were appearing in the sky, there were fans around the world watching the new video and sharing their opinion of it.

Starting at the new school has been tough but, without my vlog, it would have been awful. Nothing is better than the laughs and gossip you share with real-life friends. But if you can't have those, a thumbs up or a nice comment is a pretty good substitute.

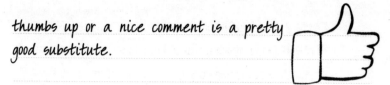

9PM

The next time Emma is free to come round is Saturday, but the fans are starting to worry and I'm not sure what to do:

 Just Being Courtney H
Don't leave us. We need you.

 Poppy M
I have been so sad I cannot eat. Please come back and tell us you are fine.

Crazy Kaitlin 2001
You are a big part of our life too, please come back to us.

10PM

I just commented on the Spring Sale Haul video as Destiny. I hope this will be enough to put the fans at ease until Friday.

The Vlogger Diaries

 Destiny

Hi guys! Thanks so much for all your awesome comments. I'm not feeling in the best place to return to the vlog right now, but I want you all to know how much your support means. Gale was my first true love and this has been really tough. But I'll get through with help from ice cream, slushy movies and you guys. My fandom really makes a difference to me. I feel like I can be myself and you won't judge. Please keep your comments coming and keep sharing my channel on Facebook and Twitter. Back soon, love you.

 Karla Turner Phillips (MachineGunKarla)

Be strong hon xxx

 Planet Kate

Proud of Destiny Channel

 Poppy M

Destiny Fam will always be there for you.

 Its Me Sophie

group hug

THURSDAY APRIL 27TH

Charlie didn't annoy me today. This is so unusual I thought I'd mention it. Most vloggers have delightful siblings with their own channels and they make adorable crossover videos. I have an overexcited little piglet who can only concentrate for more than ten seconds when he's thinking of ways to troll me.

Oh wait a moment, I spoke too soon. I can hear him laughing at videos in his room. Looks like he has managed to annoy me today after all.

Charlie's tastes are so weird. Instead of subscribing to channels to discover new stuff, he watches the same videos over and over again, and finds them just as funny every time. He always puts his speakers really loud, so I have to hear the same soundtracks booming through my wall over and over again, followed by his idiot seal laugh.

The Vlogger Diaries

The videos are:

Ultimate Fail Compilation

Bald Guy Sets His Trousers on Fire

Ostrich Attacks Girl on Pony

Skateboarding Dog

Killer Clown Scary Prank

Maybe I should set up a channel especially for idiots featuring nothing but those videos. It would be a dream for advertisers. They could reach that elusive moron market who are so dumb they'll buy anything you tell them to.

FRIDAY APRIL 28TH

Sebastian sat next to me in maths again. I kept my bag on the seat as he approached, but he put it on the floor himself.

Thanks for taking the hint, Cheese Breath.

Again he launched into boasting, as if I'd asked him to list his achievements in life so far. I managed to tune them out, but the word 'vlog' got my attention.

I asked him to repeat what he'd just said, which must have been a first for him. He told me he runs a 'massively popular' channel about first-person shooter games.

I told him to define 'massively popular' and he said some of his videos have got over 500 views.

Big whoop! My videos probably got more than that in the time it took him to brag about his so-called success.

I was trying really hard to keep quiet, but when he described himself as a 'Social Media Rock Star', I couldn't hold back.

I told him I had a vlog that regularly got 100,000 views. As soon as the words left my mouth, I wished I'd kept quiet. All I needed was for him to track down my vlog and work out Destiny was fictional, and he'd be able to blackmail me. He could ask for money, or even worse, he could make me pretend we were friends.

I backtracked right away. I said it wasn't true really and I'd just been trying to impress him because I was jealous of his amazing vlog. Then I had to distract him by asking about games until the end of the lesson.

Looking interested was really tough. I fixed a grin on my face and held my breath as he compared the strategic merits of a Weevil submachine gun and a SVG-100 sniper rifle in the new *Call of Duty* game.

Sebastian did tell me one interesting thing, though. He's not going on the New York trip. So if I do manage to make enough to go, there's no chance of getting stuck next to him on the flight. Even more reason to get the vlog to take off.

Emma's coming round tomorrow night for another video. I'm doing this one as a live stream so Destiny can be surprised by dramatic events halfway through. This means we'll have to rehearse it a few times before we go ahead, but it will be much more exciting if we pull it off.

I'd better go and announce it on Destiny's Facebook and Twitter right now.

SATURDAY APRIL 29TH

THE DESTINY CHANNEL LIVE STREAM

Hey everyone! Sorry sorry sorry about the wait.
But I'm back now and I want you all to know I'm
fine and I'm moving on. I'm going to get out there
and live my life and share it with you guys.

*[Emma did this one from the edge of the bed. This
meant viewers could see the open bedroom door behind
her.]*

Gale was a big part of my life but I'm over him now.
And it's all thanks to the help you guys gave me.
There were so many great comments I don't even
know where to start.

*[As Emma talked into the phone, Callum
appeared in the doorway holding a bunch
of flowers and the purple teddy bear
hugging the love heart. I'm glad I got to
use that eventually.]*

And thanks so much for all your messages, emails and tweets. Every single one means so much to me. You have absolutely no idea.

[Just as we rehearsed, Emma turned round and spotted Callum. She burst into tears and reached out for her camera. Then we cut the feed. Well, you've got to leave them wanting more.]

As soon as we were done, we all crowded around my monitor and watched the comments come in. Emma read them out in different accents, and it was pretty funny. But I also felt a little guilty, like we were teasing our fandom. Some fans turned up too late for the stream, so I posted it to my account to let them replay it.

Woah Kelsey
OMG What has happened after this stream ended?

Karla Turner Phillips (MachineGunKarla)
TELL ME U WILL TAKE HIM BACK. GALE AND DESTINY FOR EVER.

Just Being Courtney H
You deserve better then him.

 xxFashionGirlxx
OMG I can't even … What just happened? This was insane?

 Lothario99
Just to let you know babe, the offer of coffee is still on xxx

 xxFashionGirlxx
Ew.

 destinyisperfect
Gale and Destiny's perfection and beauty kinda hurts.

SUNDAY APRIL 30TH

AN IMPORTANT QUESTION | THE DESTINY CHANNEL

Hey guys! Thanks to all of you who watched the live stream, sorry it stopped so suddenly. For those of you who missed it, Gale came back here again. He tried to make up with me. And now … Now I don't know.

The thing is, I'm really not sure what to do. Gale made me cry for a week. I can't just take him back. But we do have a real connection. How often does that really happen? And he's admitted he made a mistake and apologized.

[I got Emma to stare into space for a few seconds and then cut to the next bit. I closed the curtains and put the light on so it looked as though she'd spent ages mulling it over.]

You know what? I need your help, guys. Leave a comment and let me know what you think I should do. Also, there's a link to a poll in the description. Should I keep Gale or should I kick him to the kerb? It's your decision, guys. Get voting!!!

Now I'm wondering if I went too far. I thought the fans would like having a say in Destiny's personal life. But maybe it's unrealistic that anyone would make such a major decision like this. I don't want the whole vlog to fall apart because of one video.

It's hard for me to tell. I've never had a boyfriend,

not really. A few boys at my old school asked me out, but they all made Sebastian look like Ryan Gosling. And I sometimes had secret crushes, but I never did anything about them. Unless forgetting how to speak/turning red/tripping over etc. when they were around counts.

9PM

I shouldn't have worried. None of the regular fans thought it was weird to make a major decision like this. In fact, the only person who thought it was at all strange was one of the regular trolls, and no one cares what he thinks:

Just Being Courtney H
No. You need a man who R E S P E C T you.

Karla Turner Phillips (MachineGunKarla)
Yes. Just thinking about you guys back together makes me emosh.

Queen Ashley III
Gale is a dog.

Its Me Sophie

Take him back! Destiny and Gale are my OTP.

 Lothario99

Seriously. Message me.

 xxFashionGirlxx

Stay classy, internet.

 Dating Fails

Still single? Check out these secrets dating websites don't want you to know bit.ly/1UHA9Zn

 Evil Liam 13

What is wrong with you? If you got run over would you hold a fan poll to decide whether to call an ambulance?

Crazy Kaitlin 2001

It's called having friends, you wouldn't understand. Take a look at your own life before hating on others.

Evil Liam 13

I DON'T WANT TO LIVE ON THIS PLANET ANYMORE.

MONDAY MAY 1ST

Grace from the Swans was off sick today, so the seat next to Emma in chemistry was free. I hung around at the back of the room, unsure if I would be allowed to sit there.

Emma seems so friendly when she comes round to make the videos now. She even arrived an hour early for the last one so I could go through her *Romeo and Juliet* audition with her. I read Romeo's lines so badly we did more laughing than rehearsing, but I hope it was still a bit useful.

She's never actually come out and said I can talk to her in school now, but I was sure it must be true.

While I was pondering this, Sebastian barged past and took the seat. I trudged forward to my usual spot on the front row.

I glanced back at Emma and Sebastian from time to time during the lesson. At first she was recoiling from him as anyone sane would, but she soon started actually talking to him. Unless she's suddenly got interested in first-person shooters, I reckon he must have been talking to her about vlogs.

That can't be good.

TUESDAY MAY 2ND

I was right. It wasn't good.

I was sitting on the table at the back of the lunch hall when Emma came over and planted her hands on her hips.

It seems Sebastian has stumbled across the Clickfeed article. He noticed how much the new vlogger called Destiny looked like Emma and watched the video.

He remembered what I'd told him in chemistry and worked out what we'd been up to.

He spent all yesterday's class stirring things up by saying that vlogs as popular as ours bring in thousands of pounds. Now Emma's convinced I'm ripping her off and is refusing to appear in any more videos unless I pay her £50 for each one.

Thanks, Cheese Breath. You just bankrupted me.

WEDNESDAY MAY 3RD

Emma won't budge on her demands, and the fans are desperate for another video. I had to return to the vlog's comments section tonight to tide them over until I can make Emma see sense.

Destiny
Hey guys. Thanks so much to everyone who's voted so far. And thanks for all your comments. I appreciate them so much, and I read every single one. I just need to ask a small favour. If you don't think I should get back with Gale, please try not to be rude about him. He's a real person with real feelings too. Anyway, I promise I'll be back soon. Keep your votes coming in.

destinyisperfect
True fans know Gale is perfect for Destiny. You are not part of this fandom if you don't.

Finn Funn
I agree that Gale is perfect for Destiny. They are both morons.

destinyisperfect
Go ahead and troll us we are the true fam we don't care LOL.

THURSDAY MAY 4TH

The seat next to Emma was free again today and this time I went straight for it. I tried to explain to her that Sebastian was talking nonsense and I'd actually been losing money on the vlog, but she wouldn't believe me.

In the end I had to log in to my bank account on my phone. I showed her all the money that had gone out and the pitiful sum that had come in. She said she's going to think about it and get back to me.

FRIDAY MAY 5TH

Sebastian was waiting at the school gates this morning. He said he'd spoken to Emma and agreed to act as her agent. He then pulled out a sheet of paper and told me it was a legal contract for us all to sign.

I brushed the bright orange crumbs off and read it. It basically said all three of us would get an equal share of any profits. Me for coming up with the vlog and writing it, Emma for performing it and Sebastian for ... oh, wait a moment ... Sebastian for absolutely nothing at all.

I screwed the paper into a ball and threw it at him.

Emma was with the Swans at lunchtime, but she came over to sit with me. Jasmine and Grace pretended to ignore us, though they kept giving us the evil side eye. Maybe hanging out with uncool people at lunchtime is an even worse crime than wearing school shoes on No Uniform Day.

I told Emma there was no point wasting a third of our profits supporting Sebastian's cheesy puffs habit. I offered to split the money evenly and give her more creative control. This last bit sounds good, but it really just means I'll let her improvise more, which she's really good at anyway. As long as she doesn't insist on including the stuff about Destiny being mute until the age of eight, we'll be fine.

So, crisis over. The evil braced one has been defeated, Emma is back on side and I can finally make another video for the fans.

SATURDAY MAY 6TH

BIG ANNOUNCMENT TA-DAH | THE DESTINY CHANNEL

Hi everyone. I'm here at last! Thanks for all your advice. Having you guys there for me meant so much. You are all my best friend in the world. Every single one of you. So I can now tell you that with your help I have decided ...

[Callum jumped into frame and shouted 'I'm back' here. He did it earlier than he was meant to, but Emma covered it well.]

Well that's my big reveal ruined. It's pretty obvious what I've decided now, isn't it?

[Callum threw his arms around Emma and kissed her on the cheek. How do actors manage to do that stuff without getting embarrassed? If Callum or anyone did it to me I'd flush bright red and have to stop the recording for a year while I calmed down.]

The fans started arguing as soon as I posted the video, just as I'd hoped.

Just Being Courtney H
Who else was waiting for this to be uploaded?

> **Queen Ashley III**
> Me.

> **My Name is Simone**
> Me too!

> **Poppy M**
> Me three!

Its Me Sophie
Gale and Destiny 4 Ever.

 Crazy Kaitlin 2001
True Destiny fans hate Gale.

> **Chloe C**
> How can you even say that? He makes Destiny happy and you would want her to be happy if u r a true fan.

> **Crazy Kaitlin 2001**
> I'm the first Destiny fan I know what is right for her.

> **Chloe C**
> I just went back and checked, I was first.

 Karla Turner Phillips (MachineGunKarla)
<3 <3 <3 Gale

 Earn$$$
I make over a thousand dollars a month responding to online surveys. Find out how at easymoneyfromhome.com

 Just Being Courtney H
Please listen to me he is not right for you trust me on this I'm so sorry but I need to say it as a friend.

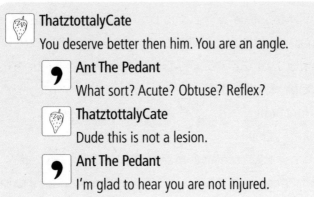

ThatztottalyCate
You deserve better then him. You are an angle.

Ant The Pedant
What sort? Acute? Obtuse? Reflex?

ThatztottalyCate
Dude this is not a lesion.

Ant The Pedant
I'm glad to hear you are not injured.

SUNDAY MAY 7TH

A SPECIAL PLEA | THE DESTINY CHANNEL

Hi guys. I've got something to ask. Please could we all stop fighting? It's great that you all had an opinion on Gale, but we've made our decision now, so let's all get behind it.

[Emma made her voice go up and down like she was just about to burst into tears, then stopped and waved her hand in front of her face.]

Sorry ... I promised myself I wouldn't. It's just that

I really want it to work this time with Gale and I need you all to do your best. But when you leave comments like 'he's not right for you' and 'true fans hate Gale' you need to know it hurts me. I'm sorry. This is not easy.

Emma spent the rest of the video reading through the comments on the last video and getting more and more upset. I thought this would be a good way to stir things up.

Just as I'd hoped, this new video got the fans going even more:

Its Me Sophie

I told you all to back Gale now she's had to come out and say this I hope you all feel good.

Queen Ashley III

I still hate Gale but I will give him my support for you Destiny even though he is a dog.

Planet Kate

Proud of you both.

Karla Turner Phillips (MachineGunKarla)
Don't listen to the comments of rude and disrespectful people. Whatever you say there will always be someone who'll argue with you.

 Flames R Us
I strongly disagree.

 中国球迷
我们是你的中国扇子，我们认为你应该干掉他

 Finn Funn
If that's Chinese for 'This vlog is stupid and everyone who follows it sucks', then I agree.

 Crazy Kaitlin 2001
I don't care what you say I still don't trust Gale
#OrginalFandom #OccupyGale

 Aaliyah H
KMT how can you be in the fandom and then go against her wishes it makes no sense.

Just Being Courtney H
You should never have taken him back your making a terrible mistake.

> **SHOUTING LAUREN**
> I AM SO ANGRY RIGHT NOW THIS IS TEARING OUR FANDOM APART THE FIRST THING WE HAVE TO DO AS FANS IS SUPPORT DESTINY IN WHAT SHES DECIDED THIS IS SO IMPORTANT TO HER YOU CANNOT CALL YOURSELF A FAN AND TALK LIKE THIS ABOUT THE MAN SHE LOVES.
>
> **Evil Liam 13**
> You sound fun.

MONDAY MAY 8TH

Destiny got her first ever reaction video tonight. A girl with dyed blonde hair and impressive false eyelashes stares at her screen while the Special Plea vlog plays in a small window in the top right of frame.

A SPECIAL PLEA – REACTION | RUBY REACTS

Okay people. There's a new Destiny video up. Let's see what she's got to say.

[Ruby stares at the screen while Emma asks the fans to stop fighting.]

Oh my god. Why would you do this to her? You're meant to be her fandom, right? Did I get that right?

[Ruby watches the screen again. The video cuts to Destiny crying and Ruby starts wiping the corners of her eyes and snivelling too.]

Look what you've done to her. Take a look at yourself, fans. Sorry, I can't do this. I just can't …

Why would you…

I'm just like …

It goes on like this until the Destiny video ends.

I guess it's flattering, and I hope it spreads the word about the vlog, but I'm really confused about why anyone watches these reaction videos.

I clicked through to Ruby Reacts' channel and saw

she had half a million subscribers. Why are so many people hooked on watching someone else watch videos? They can see her laugh at slapstick videos, retch at gross-out videos and jump at scare videos. But why not just watch the videos yourself? I don't get it.

8PM

Okay, this is weird. Someone's just posted a reaction video to the reaction video. And they seem pretty upset too. Maybe someone will react to that and someone will react to that and then the whole internet will collapse. It's making my brain hurt to think about it.

9PM

AAARRRGGHHH!

Sorry about that. I can't scream here in my room because everyone would hear, so I had to write a scream instead.

Has that got it out of my system?

No. Not quite.

AAAARRRAAAARRRRAAAARRRRAAAARRRG-
GHHH!

That's better. Ten minutes ago, Mum barged into my room and announced she'd decided to start a vlog too, because she can see how much I'm enjoying mine. Then she took her phone out and played a video on it.

Like a deer frozen in the headlights of a truck, I was unable to run and save myself. The video was so awful I'm trying to force it out of my mind, but it keeps coming back. Why isn't there a delete function for my memory?

Mum shot it in portrait mode, which wasn't a surprise. This means the video would be either sideways or too narrow online. Why do phones even give people the option to do that?

But at least she'd pointed her phone the right way. She once came back from a day trip with fifty

accidental selfies because she hadn't realized her phone was on front camera.

The first five minutes of the video showed Mum describing her day in mind-numbing detail. She said she'd loaded the dishwasher, driven to work, microwaved some soup and gone to her amateur dramatics class.

Just as the video was sending me to sleep, she started singing 'I Feel Pretty' from *West Side Story*. Like any expert torturer, she'd lulled me into a false sense of security before unleashing the real pain.

Mum asked me to upload her video. After a quick search I found an unpopular Chinese site called PowerVideoTube and put it on there instead. It really is the kindest thing to do. She has no idea how brutally honest people are online.

I may have saved millions of people from experiencing my pain, but now I'm worried about any Chinese people who accidentally watch it. I hope this doesn't lead to some sort of international crisis.

TUESDAY MAY 9TH

The last two videos are now up to 200,000 views. My plan to turn Destiny and Gale into a soap opera is working. But I need the next twist in their story.

Hmm.

Idea one — Gale dies in a tragic accident. He could be carrying a huge flammable love-heart teddy bear to her house when a stray firework hits him.

No, that would be too much. I want the fans to be gripped, not traumatized.

Idea two — Destiny dumps Gale. She changes her mind and gives in to the Gale-haters.

No. Half the fans still really like Gale. I don't want them to turn against Destiny and desert the vlog.

Idea three — Destiny thinks Gale is trying to kill her. She finds some poison in his coat and asks the fans if she should go to the police.

Definitely no. I stole that idea from a daytime soap opera I watched when I had the flu. I think it might have ended with the main character dying and coming back as a ghost, though that could have been a dream brought on by my high temperature.

Idea four — Gale has another girlfriend he isn't telling Destiny about.

That's the one! I can plant clues for Destiny to worry about, like perfume on Callum's clothes or lipstick on his collar. The fans will watch the videos over and over again and argue in the comments section, boosting the view counts. Perfect.

Emma's coming round tomorrow, so I'll get working on the script.

WEDNESDAY MAY 10TH

MOUTH FULL OF WATER CHALLENGE | THE DESTINY CHANNEL

Hi guys! Guess who's back ... Guess who's back ... Galey's back ... Galey's back. Ta-dah!

And it's a new challenge. Here's how it goes. One of us fills their mouth with water while the other chooses a funny vid. If we can resist laughing, we get a point. But if we laugh and water goes everywhere, the other person gets a point. And if we laugh so much water goes all over the computer, it will break and that will be the end of this vlog. So let's not do that.

[At this point Callum took a sip of water, but looked at Emma and laughed it out straight away. I was lucky they were both in a giddy mood when we made this.]

That's a point to me! I've already got a point and we haven't even started yet. Okay, here comes my first video: 'Lizard Jumps on News Guy'.

[As soon as Callum started watching the video, he got the giggles and spat water down the front of his hoodie. By the end of the video it looked like they'd had a water fight.]

I uploaded this video and watched with Emma as the likes and comments came in.

Aleksandra Love Heart
<3 <3 <3 Destiny and Gale

destinyisperfect
Sooooooooooooooooooooooo cute together.

Koharu99
It is my birthday today.

Jodie Creates
Check out my Destiny and Gale fanfic at bit.ly/29d1ZPc

Evil Liam 13
You need help.

After about an hour, we went back on with a surprise live update:

THE DESTINY CHANNEL LIVE STREAM

Hi guys. Loving the comments, keep them coming. Sorry to put this on you, but I'm worried and I thought you might be able to help. Gale left his hoodie here after we made the video earlier and

I was just hanging it up when I smelled perfume on it. It's not one I've ever used, which makes me wonder how the smell got on there. Maybe he's using a new sort of washing powder or something. But it really smells like perfume. Do you think I should ask him about it? Or will that make me seem crazy and jealous?

Emma went on like this for about ten minutes, improvising but thankfully not including any ridiculous backstories. The comments came in so fast it was hard to read them:

> **Pretty Much Just Me**
> Call Gale right now and ask him what was the perfume. Don't let him watch this and have time to come up with an excuse.
>
> **My Life As Alex**
> Actually this is a private matter and we should leave Destiny to work through it on her own.
>
> **Pretty Much Just Me**
> Wrong. This affects the whole of the fandom.

Crazy Kaitlin 2001

Gale is cheating on you like I said, get rid of him. Where else would perfume come from except his other girlfriend?

My Name is Simone

I know Gale would never do anything to hurt you there must be an explanation for this I need to think straight oh my god.

Planet Kate

Destiny pls read out my comments!!!

Chloe C

OMG this is worrying I don't even

Finn Funn

... know how to finish sentences.

THURSDAY MAY 11TH

I sat next to Emma in chemistry today and she didn't tell me to go away. In fact, we had such a good chat about the vlog that Mr Williams had to tell us to be quiet.

Check me getting in trouble for talking. That's the closest thing to social success I've had since starting at this school.

Emma still ignores me when she's with Jasmine and Grace, but when they're not around she's absolutely fine.

So I've officially made a part—time friend. That's better than nothing. I think.

FRIDAY MAY 12TH

Sebastian sat next to me at lunch today and boasted about his vlog again.

Really? He tries to rip me off one minute and the next he thinks we can be best friends?

But I let him drone on. If I get on the wrong side of him, I'm sure he'll come up with a plan to blackmail us into paying him loads of money to keep the truth about the vlog secret. I need to keep him thinking we're all still friends so his mind doesn't turn to revenge.

So I had to smile and nod. I just hope no one thought I was talking to him because we're dating. There'd be no way back from that social shame.

SATURDAY MAY 13TH

THE DESTINY CHANNEL LIVE STREAM

Just a quick update for everyone who watched the other night. Forget everything I said. I've checked with Gale and he lent his hoodie to his sister. That's why it smelled of perfume. I feel kind of stupid for even mentioning it. But I didn't make a big deal about it – I just said it in the middle of some other stuff. Anyway, I've put my mind at rest now. Thanks for all your comments, keep them coming in …

As the live stream went on, massive arguments broke out in the comments section.

Crazy Kaitlin 2001

I don't see why you would believe him. Who would wear their brother's clothes anyway? Ew.

 Chloe C

OMG she has just stopped worrying. Why would you even say this?

 Crazy Kaitlin 2001

Destiny please read this call his sister and see if she borrowed his hoodie. Then you'll know.

 My Life As Alex

So happy you and Gale have worked it out.

 Crazy Kaitlin 2001

You seriously think that's happened???

 Sarah Sarcasm

Seems Legit.

 destinyisperfect

So so happy. Destiny and Gale together is the most beautiful thing I've ever seen.

 Finn Funn

In that case you can't have seen that video where a cat dressed as a shark rides a vacuum cleaner.

SUNDAY MAY 14TH

Mum came into my room this evening and chucked her phone on to my desk. She said there was a new vlog on it, and I should take it off and put it on the internet. Then she went out, leaving me to 'enjoy' the video.

I uploaded it to the same Chinese site as before and watched with my finger over the mute button. I needed to be ready to act in a split second if any more singing broke out.

If possible, the video was even worse than the last. Mum spent the whole time moaning about how we never get together as a family anymore. She said her daughter spends too long on her computer and she wishes she'd come down and chat more often. Then she said she should at least tidy her room once in a while if she insists on spending so long in it.

Yeah, Mum, I can see what you're up to. You think that by putting your usual moans in a vlog, I'll be more likely to pay attention to them. Well I won't. I even threw a couple of extra socks on the floor to prove I hadn't listened.

Mum came back a few minutes later to collect her phone and asked me what the internet thought of the video. I told her the internet thought people should be allowed to stay in their rooms if they wanted to and if other people were so offended by the state of their rooms they should stop barging in all the time. Mum said the internet sounded like it had a lot of growing up to do.

MONDAY MAY 15TH

I heard someone approaching as I walked home today. I was worried it might be Sebastian, but it turned out to be Emma. She didn't even look ashamed to be with me. We must have been well out of sight of the Swans.

I suggested we go to the high street and pick out some clothes for the next haul video instead of heading straight home. I thought shopping for clothes might be less stressful with her there, but it didn't turn out that way.

We were looking through a rack of sale jumpers when I spotted a couple of girls pointing and giggling from the other side of the store.

Maybe I'm paranoid, okay definitely I'm paranoid, but my first thought was that they were coming over to tease me about my clothes or my hair or something. I always felt out of place in those shops.

But it wasn't me they were interested in. They barged up to Emma and said, 'Oh my god, you're Destiny.' Emma switched straight into bitchy face, as if Sebastian had approached her while she was with the Swans. She pushed past the fans and walked away without saying anything.

I suppose I should have seen this coming, as the vlog is getting so popular. I keep thinking of the view count like a high score on a computer game, and forgetting there are real people behind it. Emma was bound to bump into some eventually.

If I'd thought about it, I could have prepared her. I'd have told her to hug each fan and squeal, just as Destiny would. Now these poor fans would go straight on Facebook and Twitter and spread the word that Destiny was nasty in real life.

I dashed over to Emma and told her we were going to do a drama exercise. She had to imagine the girls she'd just blanked were old friends she was meeting for the first time in months. She instantly switched into Destiny mode and went back over to them. I've got to hand it to her, she knows how to commit to a role.

She greeted them, chatted and even posed for selfies, which is great because the fans will share them online and spread the word about the vlog. What could have been a PR disaster became a triumph. I'm so glad I was there.

I wish I could act. I'd get myself into character as a confident, friendly, popular girl and stay in it forever.

TUESDAY MAY 16TH

Callum was out of breath when he arrived to record the new video tonight. He said he'd been outside Starbucks with his girlfriend when a group of angry girls ran over from the other side of the street and started yelling. They'd called him a cheater and one of them had thrown fries at him. Callum and his girlfriend Megan had to escape by jumping on a bus.

I really hope that was nothing to do with the vlog. You sometimes see gangs of girls in the town centre, so it could have been a random attack. A girl from school got her phone stolen by some a couple of weeks ago. But the stuff about cheating makes me think they're Destiny fans.

I feel sort of guilty, especially as the video we've just made stirs thing up even more …

WORD CHALLENGE | THE DESTINY CHANNEL

Hey guys! Welcome back. It's word association challenge time! Yay! It's very simple. I say a word, then Gale says a related word, then I say another related word. We keep going until one of us pauses or repeats a word or says one that has nothing to do with the last.

I used to play this with my friend Steph. It would always end in an argument about which words were related to which. She once refused to speak to me for a week because I wouldn't let her follow 'plastic bag' with 'motorbike' because 'they were both things she'd seen in the street'.

Sometimes the best videos happen by mistake. My original idea for this one was for lipstick to fall out of Gale's pocket on to the floor. Destiny would fail to spot it, so the fans could point it out to her in the comments. But what happened was much more convincing.

I got Emma and Callum to play the challenge for real, as I thought it would be easier than writing a script. After a couple of minutes, Callum got to the word 'friend' and Emma said 'girlfriend'. By this time, they were both genuinely saying the first things that came into their minds. So Callum said 'Megan' — the name of his actual girlfriend.

Instead of continuing, Emma asked Callum why he hadn't said her name instead. Callum said it was a mistake, and Emma looked really confused. I'm so glad they both managed to stay in character.

They continued with the game and Emma made no mention of Gale's slip when she did her usual wrap-up asking the fans to comment and subscribe.

I uploaded the video an hour ago and already even the most loyal Gale fans are turning against him:

Crazy Kaitlin 2001

And finally the truth comes out. Let me say this to you as a friend – Gale is cheating on you with a girl called Megan, now you have your proof, END IT.

Queen Ashley III

Gale's face at 3:14 check out the guilt.

Chloe C

So what? It doesn't prove anything, that could be the name of his ex.

Just Being Courtney H

And that's the first name in his mind? Still not cool.

Aleksandra Love Heart

I'm sorry to say I voted to keep U with Gale. I admit I was wrong, now you must admit it too.

Jaydenisonfire

I was just about to go to bed when this came through now I will not sleep *sigh*

ThatztottalyCate

what is this cannot be write if hes says her name then cant be good fr you just feels wrong

Finn Funn

I'm fluent in moron. Please allow me to translate. "I believe your boyfriend is untrustworthy."

WEDNESDAY MAY 17TH

It's here! An email with a link to my new ad revenue payment. Not sure I want to know. Okay ... I'm going to look ...

£463.46

That's okay, I think. If it stays the same next month, I should have just enough to cover the New York trip once I've given Emma her share. Mission accomplished. Then I can delete the channel and all of Destiny's social media accounts and move on.

THURSDAY MAY 18TH

Oops. This message has just come through to Destiny's account:

Hi Destiny, we saw your so-called boyfriend Gale with ANOTHER GIRL yesterday. We wanted to get a picture to prove it, but he ran away. My friend Tracey hit him with a French fry tho LOL.

It looks like the girls who chased Callum were Destiny fans. What kind of a rabid mob have I created? If they track Callum down and kill him, will I have to go to prison too?

It's fine. I'll be deleting the vlog as soon as I get enough for the New York trip. I just hope for Callum's sake he doesn't run into these girls again before then. They sound scary.

FRIDAY MAY 19TH

Emma sat with me instead of the Swans at lunch today. I told her about the ad money and she seemed happy. Then she went through some of her ideas for the vlog, one of which was to build up the character of Gale's secret girlfriend Megan following Callum's accidental mention of her.

She even wanted Megan herself to appear in one of the videos, but I managed to talk her out of it. I'm already worried enough for her safety after the French fry incident. The fans would destroy her if they recognized her in the street.

Instead, I'm going to call Callum's phone and pretend to be Megan during the next video they do together. This way we can keep the cheating storyline going without putting Megan herself in any more danger.

I noticed a few people glancing at us as we chatted and I felt like my coolness level was finally rising.

Unfortunately, Sebastian came over to sit with us and sent it crashing right back down again.

He asked if we were talking about vlogging and if we needed his help. Emma switched to bitchy resting face and turned away. I should have at least said something to him, but I couldn't help myself. I blanked him too.

I know, I know. I did exactly what the Swans did to me. I can't complain about others being cliquey if I act the same given the first chance.

Now I'm convinced Sebastian is going to come up with a blackmail scheme. Any day now I'll find him waiting at the school gates, demanding so much money that I'll never be able to afford the school trip.

Please please please let him get distracted by a new game so he forgets all about us.

SATURDAY MAY 20TH

I knew something like this would happen. This morning Emma stepped out of her house to be greeted by a gang of rabid fans. It turns out the girls we saw on Monday followed her home and found out where she lived. This morning they came back with all their friends, assuming Destiny would want to hang out with them. But Emma was so freaked out she found it impossible to act friendly. She tried to get away from them, but they stalked after her.

The result was complete meltdown. She ended up yelling at them for being a bunch of creepy losers.

She was right, I guess. The fans were pretty creepy for going round to her house. But when you've watched someone speaking to you directly from your screen, it's easy to forget you don't know them.

If Emma could have kept calm and explained this in friendly Destiny mode, they might have been okay with it. As it is we could have a major backlash on our hands.

Soon after, Emma called me and said she was resigning from the vlog. I managed to talk her back round by saying it's great training for when she's a famous actress and the paparazzi come after her.

Now we need a new video to limit the damage before any of the fans she insulted can spread the word.

SUNDAY MAY 21ST

AN APOLOGY | THE DESTINY CHANNEL

Hey guys. I've got something to say to you all today, and it's going to be difficult for me. That's because it's never easy to admit you're wrong.

Yesterday morning I stepped out of my front door to be greeted by a large group of fans. Although it was wrong of them to find out my address and come to my house, I should still have taken the time to thank them for their support. Instead, I was rude to them.

It's not like me to behave that way, and I'm very sorry. The last couple of days have been very difficult for me.

[Emma then picked up Loki, who squirmed against her and scowled. I turned the vacuum on just before recording the video to make sure he'd be in a foul mood.]

I had to take Loki to the vet on Friday to get tested for pneumonia. Luckily, he was fine, but he was pretty shaken by it as you can see. I was very stressed too, and that's why I wasn't acting like myself. I promise it won't happen again.

[Emma added 'but don't ever come to my house again', but I edited it out so the video ended on a positive note.]

I didn't think this video would be as exciting as the Gale ones, but the view count leapt up to almost 20,000 right away. The hardcore fanbase would probably watch Destiny washing up right now.

And the comment section was as busy as ever:

My Life As Alex

We forgive you. It's no wonder you were worried with poor Loki suffering like that.

Queen Ashley III

Who were these freaks turning up at your house anyway? That's crossing a line.

Evil Liam 13

Don't get a channel if you don't want to become a famous vlogger.

Queen Ashley III

You have a channel. Would you like it if I turned up at your house?

Evil Liam 13

Sure. My address is Your Butt, 15 Your Butt Street, Your Buttchester.

Pixie Sunshine YAY

Name and shame those who didn't respect your privacy.

Finn Funn

But that wouldn't be respecting their privacy.

Planet Kate

#stillproudofdestiny

Crazy Life XD
You acted wrong but at least you have apologized so let's move on. What is your home address please?

Aleksandra Love Heart
I know you're stressed about Loki's illness but don't let it distract you from the truth about Gale. Please listen to us.

MONDAY MAY 22ND

A lot of fans are messaging Destiny and asking for her address. Weird that the thing they're taking from the last video is that it's fine to call round.

On the other hand, it should give us a really good excuse to end the Destiny vlog when we need to. She could announce in a final tearful video that too many fans have invaded her privacy, leaving her with no choice but to quit.

9PM

Mum burst into my room just now and demanded to

know how her vlogs were doing. I said they were fine, but she insisted I check. I logged back on to the Chinese site and was astonished to see they actually were doing quite well. They'd both been viewed over 4000 times and had over 300 likes. There were a few comments too, but when I tried putting them through Google translate they all turned out to be fake handbag spam. Mum said they might be suggesting handbags to go with her outfit and that we should click the links. Ever wondered why spam still exists and who could possibly be stupid enough to fall for it? There's your answer.

I genuinely can't explain Mum's Chinese fanbase. Maybe a teacher somewhere in China set her video as homework for an English lesson. But that wouldn't explain why four thousand people would all subject themselves to her version of 'I Feel Pretty'. Very strange.

Do they even have vlogs in China? Mum might be the only Western vlogger they know. What if she becomes a social media superstar and we're besieged by coach parties demanding autographs and selfies? At least I'll find out if it's possible to die of embarrassment.

TUESDAY MAY 23RD

BLINDFOLD MAKEUP CHALLENGE | THE DESTINY CHANNEL

Hey guys! Gale's in for a treat, because I'm doing his makeup today. And I'll be wearing a blindfold just to pile on the agony. You agreed to this, Galey. You've only got yourself to blame.

[I then cut to Emma wearing the blindfold and groping around on the desk. She grabbed a tube of lipstick and daubed it around Callum's mouth in a wide circle. She added layer after layer of makeup until he looked like something drawn by a child after too many sugary drinks.]

How is he looking? I think he needs just a touch more mascara. Don't forget to leave a comment and let me know what you thought.

[At this point I went outside and rang Callum. He said he couldn't talk, ended the call and shot a quick guilty look at the camera. Emma kept on daubing makeup on his face and laughing, but Callum looked much more shifty and serious.]

After this, pretty much the entire fandom was against Gale:

 Poppy M
Listen to the call from 5:23 to 5:30. If you turn the volume up you can hear a girl saying, 'Hi it's me, just wondering what time you'd be back.' This must be Megan.

 Crazy Kaitlin 2001
You need to get rid of Gale. Pls reply to this Destiny we need to know you are reading.

 Isabella365
OMG did he just? Sorry, I can't.

 Chloe C
I was team Gale but I was wrong. Sorry.

WEDNESDAY MAY 24TH

Destiny got a message from someone called Emily today. She said she was a researcher, so I guessed she had another dodgy product to promote. I was about to delete it when I saw Emily worked for a television show called *Talking Point* that features discussions of hot topics with expert guests and a studio audience. This week they're discussing vloggers, and they want Destiny and some of her biggest fans to go on.

At first I was worried about Emma appearing on TV as Destiny, but when I Googled the show I saw it was just on a local station, so it's not like millions of people would see her. But it would make a good subject for a vlog and if it goes well I can upload it as a bonus video. I'll see what Emma thinks.

9PM

I heard the same piece of weird music playing over and over again this evening. I guessed Charlie had found a new video to add to his favourites.

Then half an hour ago, Mum came in and announced she'd made a new video especially for her Chinese fans.

She'd found a video called 'Chinese Umbrella Dance' and decided to recreate it. It might have helped if she'd used a pretty, colourful dance umbrella rather than the broken grey one from under the stairs. It might also have helped if Charlie hadn't been pointing and giggling in the background. But nothing could have helped it really.

I think those sort of dances are meant to feature lots of people in perfect sync. Ten people tiptoeing and twirling umbrellas on stage is impressive. One person doing it in their living room looks insane.

Mum should have taken a hint from my facepalm reaction. But no, she insisted I upload it to PowerVideoTube. I just hope China doesn't think she was mocking their traditions and launch a cyberattack on us.

THURSDAY MAY 25TH

I sat next to Emma at lunch today and told her all about the TV show. Right away, she said she wanted to do it. She's always wanted to be on TV, and you'd think she'd been offered the leading role in an international drama series from the way she was squealing. It's a step up from nasty health-shake commercials, I suppose.

She promised she could stay in character the whole time, even when I warned her that the interviewer might give her a tough time.

I just messaged Emily back and accepted. I'm still not 100% sure it's going to work, but at least we've got the rest of the week to prepare.

8PM

Mum's dance video has already had a thousand views and it's even generated a response video. It features a middle-aged woman talking really quickly for five minutes. I can't work out if she's angry or happy. But let's just assume she's accusing Mum of insulting her nation and forbidding her from making a video ever again.

FRIDAY MAY 26TH

The TV show goes out live from noon on Sunday. Destiny's segment will be last, and she'll be on for ten minutes. The interviewer is called Seema Osman, and she doesn't seem too fearsome from what I could find of her online. She'll probably ask Emma if vlogs are warping the minds of innocent young people, because that's the sort of stupid thing they ask on those shows.

Emily asked if Destiny could recommend some superfans to be in the audience for the show, so I gave my own name and said I'd put out a call in the vlog's comments section to find the others. I really hope none of the ones Emma was rude to turn up.

I can't believe I've just volunteered to go on TV. I must be one of the only people in the world who's never wanted to. I couldn't even watch back my one attempt at recording myself for a vlog. The idea of having my face beamed into living rooms makes me feel queasy.

But I've got to be there for Emma's interview. After Seema Osman has spoken to her, she wants the fans to ask questions. If I'm one of them, we can prepare in advance and there's less chance things will go wrong.

SATURDAY MAY 27TH

TV NERVES | THE DESTINY CHANNEL

Hey guys. I'm feeling very nervous today and the reason is because ... wait for it ... I'm going on *Talking Point* tomorrow. Squee!

I know, I know. What I'm doing right now isn't so different from being on TV. I'm sure some of you watch this channel through your smart TVs anyway.

But when I record this, I feel like I'm chatting with a friend. And I am. You're all my best friend, like I've said.

Tomorrow I'll be in a studio with an audience and cameras and lights and microphones. It's giving me butterflies just thinking about it.

So keep your fingers crossed for me. Wish me luck in the comments, watch the show if you can, and thanks so much to all the superfans who are coming along tomorrow to support me.

[Emma lifted her hands to the camera to show her fingers were crossed and made a squealing noise.]

After we posted the video, I made Emma answer
some questions that might come up tomorrow:

Why is vlogging so popular right now?
How did you get started?
What advice would you give to someone setting
up their own vlog?
What is the best type of video to make?
Do you think vlogs will turn your generation into
dribbling zombies who can only express themselves
in emojis?

I'm glad we practised. At first Emma treated it
like a drama-class exercise and invented a silly
backstory about Destiny being imprisoned in an attic
by her evil stepmother, discovering an ancient
camcorder and learning to express herself through
video diaries. Everyone will realize Destiny's a fake
character if she comes out with nonsense like that
on TV.

I helped Emma prepare some sensible answers, and we
went through them over and over again like they
were lines from a play.

When she'd gone I read the comments on today's video. Unsurprisingly, most of the fans still wanted to talk about Gale rather than the show:

Crazy Kaitlin 2001
Sorry did you even see my comment on the last video? You say you read every single comment. What will you do about Gale?

Aleksandra Love Heart
Good luck <3 <3 <3

Poppy M
I don't care about your TV show, what is happening with Gale? Did you even listen back to the call in your last video yet?

Finn Funn
When is this show on? I need to make absolutely, positively sure I don't see it.

Queen Ashley III
Dump Gale or I am done with this fandom.

Chloe C
OMG that is so disrespectful. NONE of us know what she is really going through. She should dump Gale tho.

Tonight I prepared my question for the show. Instead of just asking one thing about Gale, I'm going to confront Emma with all the evidence about Gale — the phone call, the perfume, the word association game. She'll pretend to be upset and refuse to answer.

It will make sure the video is popular with the fans when I upload it to the channel, it will be a good ad for any TV viewers who've never seen the vlog and it will mean we can take up most of the question time with stuff we've prepared.

9PM

Destiny's account just received a new message:

Hi Destiny you don't know me but I live not far from you. Although I have never seen you I saw Gale in town today with another girl and he kissed her on the lips. I shot footage on my phone. My camera is no good because Mum won't let me upgrade, but I promise it was him. I'm sorry you have to find out like this and I did consider not telling you. But I don't think it was right to hold it back and that's why I'm sending it, not to stir. Now you have the evidence you should get rid of him. I don't mind if you use this footage in your vlog. Thanks, Natasha G.

The attached video was shot from the balcony in the shopping centre. It showed Callum greeting his girlfriend Megan with a kiss before queuing at the coffee stand. I'm sure it was him, but the video was grainy enough and the camera unsteady enough that it might just possibly have been someone else.

I'll definitely take Natasha up on her offer to use it in the vlog. Destiny can introduce it and say she's not sure if the footage is really Gale and ask the fans to give their opinion. The comments will go crazy and the view count will rocket again, I'm sure.

SUNDAY MAY 28TH

I got home from the TV studio at three. The first thing I did was delete Destiny's channel. Then I went to bed, pulled the covers over my head and tried not to think about what happened. It's seven now and I'm still too scared to look at my phone or computer. I can't deal with it yet.

I had to be quiet on the bus to the studio so Emma could get herself into character. I felt like I should be getting into character as a superfan too, but I was so nervous about going on TV I couldn't think straight. I was really starting to regret giving myself such a long question to remember.

We checked into reception and they gave us name badges and told us to go up to the green room at the end of the corridor. The room at the end wasn't green, but it was full of sofas, snacks and other people with name badges, so we knew it was the right place.

Emma was taken to makeup while I examined the snacks. I couldn't believe I was surrounded by free

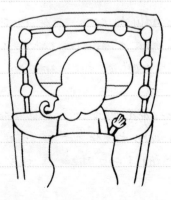

crisps, chocolates and sandwiches when I was too nervous to eat them. Just my luck.

A woman with a clipboard asked if I wanted to sit in the audience with the rest of the superfans, but I said I'd rather wait with Destiny. She said I was very lucky to be friends with a celebrity and I had this mad moment where I wanted to tell her I'd written all the words to the vlog and I was as much Destiny as Emma was. Luckily, it passed. I don't know what came over me.

Emma soon came back from makeup and we watched as the clipboard woman came in and took people to the studio. There was a woman with grey hair who was an expert on climate change and a bald man who didn't believe in it. They were really friendly to each other in the green room, but had a massive row as soon as they went in front of the cameras.

Next a middle-aged man in a suit and a woman in a purple dress were taken out to talk about house prices or something. I saw them on the screen above the green room door, but I didn't listen. I was too busy rehearsing my question over and over in my head.

Eventually the clipboard woman came in for us. She led us down a long corridor to a black curtain, pulled it back and told Emma to sit on the stool opposite Seema. Then she pointed out a gap in the front row of the audience where I had to sit.

I wished Emma luck and darted over to my seat. The studio looked smaller than it does on screen, but there was still room for ten rows of audience behind me.

Emma perched on her stool, arranged her hair and placed her hands on her lap. She went into Destiny mode as soon as the interview began. All the questions Seema asked were ones we'd prepared for, and Emma reeled off her answers perfectly.

It was all going so well. I should have guessed disaster was on the way. I was concentrating on Emma so much I barely even noticed the weird smell wafting over from behind me.

After a few minutes of chat with Emma, Seema picked up a large wireless microphone and stepped over to the audience. She asked if any of the fans had a question and I shot my hand up.

This was it. The moment I'd been preparing for all day.

A cameraman rushed over to me and shoved his lens in my face. I could see my huge face on a screen high above us. I thought I looked nervous and that made me feel nervous.

My heart was racing, my palms were sweaty and my mouth was dry.

Seema held the microphone in front of me. Over her shoulder I could see Emma smiling at me. She'd done her bit, now it was my turn.

Above me I could still see my own face. It didn't seem to be speaking. And what was that smell? It was driving me mad.

All morning I'd been running through my question. I had every word of it fixed in my mind. The perfume, the word association game, the phone call. These words were all floating around in my mind, but I had no idea how to string them together.

I think I managed to say the word 'perfume' before Seema said she'd come back to me and asked who else had a question.

'I do,' said a voice from the back of the audience. As I was wondering where I'd heard it before I suddenly worked out what the smell was.

It was cheesy puffs.

I whipped my head round and saw Sebastian. He was standing on the back row and holding his hand out for the microphone. He was wearing a black *Call of Duty* t-shirt that was tucked into his crumpled blue jeans.

No doubt he'd seen the call for fans I'd put out and got in touch with the researcher. But why had he come? I really hoped he wasn't trying to promote his own stupid vlog.

'I've got a question,' he said, snatching the mic from Seema. 'Why do you pretend to be called "Destiny" when really you're an actress called Emma Wilson? Why do you pretend Callum Smith is your boyfriend and that his name is Gale? Don't you feel you're being dishonest to your fans?'

Sebastian turned to look at me and grinned. His braces glinted under the studio lights.

I felt myself sinking down in my chair. I tried to think of something I could say that would make it better. But the only things that came into my head were perfume, word association and phone call.

Sebastian handed the mic back to Seema and sat down again.

Emma's smile dropped and her cheeks went red. She was silent for a few seconds, then she pointed at me.

'It was all Olivia's idea,' she said. 'She told me what to do.'

Seema paced back down the stairs and thrust her mic at me. The cameraman ran back over and crouched down in front of me. 'Are these allegations true?' asked Seema.

I felt like I'd plunged down a steep drop. I hadn't even managed to repeat a question I'd been preparing all day. What chance did I have of justifying the whole Destiny thing on the spot?

I felt a bead of sweat trickling down my forehead. This was going to look soooooo attractive in HD.

'Kind of,' I said. 'But I didn't mean for any of this to happen. It just got out of hand.'

I heard a sob next to me and turned to see a young girl wearing a thin jumper and green dress, just like the ones Destiny had recommended in the last haul video.

Seema strode over to her. 'You're one of Destiny's army of superfans,' she said. 'How does it feel to know you've been lied to?'

'Awful,' said the girl, wiping her eye on her sleeve. 'I thought I could trust her.'

Now I thought of something I could say. I could explain that we hadn't hurt anyone, stolen any money or even lied about anything major. We'd just created a character people felt they knew, the same as the writer of a soap opera might. I wanted to say I was sorry we'd got carried away, but what we'd done wasn't really that bad. But I didn't get the chance to say anything else.

Seema returned to her desk at the front and said they were out of time. Emma was still in shot, but she was slumping down on her stool and covering her face. Her second TV appearance had been even more embarrassing than the health milkshake ad.

The clipboard woman announced the show had gone off air and a wide door at the side of the studio opened. The audience around me began shuffling out. Emma followed them without even speaking to me.

Sebastian sauntered down from his seat on the back row and stopped in front of me on his way out.

'If only Destiny had taken on an agent,' he said. 'None of this would have happened.'

I was still too stunned to say anything more than, 'Shut up, Cheese Breath.'

The studio emptied out until there was just me and the TV crew left. Seema was standing over by her desk and gathering her papers.

'Thanks so much for that,' she said. 'That was a great piece.'

I'm glad someone enjoyed it, because it was the worst moment of my life.

MONDAY MAY 29TH

Mum and Dad didn't see the show, unsurprisingly.
This means I won't have to put up with any lectures,
but it also means I have to keep up my normal
routine so they don't realize anything's wrong.

So I went into school today, even though I felt like
staying in bed and sleeping until next year.

It wasn't that bad at first. No one mentioned the
TV disaster, and why would they? Who would be
watching a discussion show on a local station anyway?

But word soon spread. By the time I walked down the
corridor to the lunch hall, three different people
turned their phones round to show they were watching
the clip of our appearance.

Someone must have been sharing it. And you can bet
that someone has braces stuffed with bright orange
crumbs.

I took my place at the back of the queue, but a boy from the year below me turned round and shouted 'perfume'. I decided I wasn't that hungry.

I trudged away to the library, hid behind the shelf at the back and ate my bag of M&M's as quietly as I could.

My life in this school is over now. I've deleted the Destiny account and I'll never get any more ad revenue from it. But even if I did I wouldn't go on the New York trip. Anyone I tried to make friends with would just ask me about the TV disaster.

I'll just have to stick it out for a couple more years and then I can go to college where no one has seen the clip of my appearance and no one thinks it's hilarious to shout 'perfume' at me.

TUESDAY MAY 30TH

I couldn't stop myself. I checked online for the clip tonight. I was worried someone might have uploaded it so Destiny's fans could find out why her channel has suddenly gone missing.

Someone had. And no prizes for guessing who.

The clip was right at the top of Sebastian's channel, just above 'Halo 5 Full Walkthrough With Expert Commentary'. He'd named it 'The Truth About Destiny the Vlogger — You Won't Believe What She Reveals'. Nice clickbait title, Cheese Breath.

None of his other videos had more than 1000 views, but the Destiny clip was already over 10,000.

I tried to ignore the comments, but it was no use:

Crazy Kaitlin 2001
I feel like I'm actually going to be sick why would someone do this to us?

Sebastian Gamer King
So sorry about what has happened to you. Please check out my other videos and subscribe to my channel.

Ella D

I was never in the Destiny fandom but I have just learned of this and I am destroyed for you all.

 Sebastian Gamer King

So sorry about what has happened to you. Please check out my other videos and subscribe to my channel.

 Chloe C

Literally I am crying.

 Sebastian Gamer King

So sorry about what has happened to you. Please check out my other videos and subscribe to my channel.

 Evil Liam 13

All the time I was trolling the Destiny channel, it turns out I was the one being trolled. Fair play, ladies, fair play.

 Sebastian Gamer King

So sorry about what has happened to you. Please check out my other videos and subscribe to my channel.

Koharu99
I have plane tickets to come and visit Destiny's house, now what will I do?

 Sebastian Gamer King
So sorry about what has happened to you. Please check out my other videos and subscribe to my channel.

Yeah right, Sebastian. I'm sure pasting the same reply to every comment will work. Because the ideal thing to replace Destiny's vlog is two hours of a nerd explaining why a sniper rifle is better than a rocket launcher for killing zombies. Idiot.

WEDNESDAY MAY 31ST

I brought in a packed lunch today and ate it at the back of the lunch hall with my headphones on.

I was chewing some Doritos in time with my music when I felt someone nudging my arm. I looked up, preparing for someone to make yet another hilarious comment about perfume. But it was Emma.

She told me she'd been officially thrown out of the Swans. Too many people were teasing her about the TV show and Jasmine was worried the shame might rub off on them. They've let a girl called Bethany join instead, and she's been waiting to become a member for years.

I apologized to Emma for getting her into such a mess, but she said it didn't matter and she was sure everyone would forget about it all soon. But by then there was a crowd of students pointing and laughing at us, so we had to leave.

THURSDAY JUNE 1ST

Sebastian's video of our TV disaster has topped 50,000 views. It's even earned another reaction video.

THE TRUTH ABOUT DESTINY THE VLOGGER – YOU WON'T BELIEVE WHAT SHE REVEALS | RUBY REACTS

Okay, I've watched the Destiny Channel before. It

got deleted a few days ago and everyone wants to know what happened. Apparently this video explains it. Let's watch.

[As with the last video, Ruby was staring at the screen while the footage from the TV show played in a small window in the top right.]

She's on a local TV show talking about her vlog. What am I missing here? How does this explain why she deleted her channel?

[Ruby stared at the screen in confusion. The TV footage got to the bit where I was meant to ask my question. I didn't want to watch it, so I covered up the top right of the frame.]

Perfume? What does this girl mean about perfume? I don't understand, guys. Can someone tell me what I'm looking at? Okay, a guy with braces is asking a question now ...

[Ruby stared at the screen with her mouth hanging open as Sebastian made his pathetic little speech.]

I'm sorry ... What is this? It was fake? The whole thing was fake? Why would you do this to your fandom? Sorry, I can't do this. I just can't ...

[Ruby pulled out a tissue and dabbed the corner of her eye. It's no wonder she was so upset. She'd spent a whole five minutes of her life watching Destiny's videos, after all.]

This time I felt like recording a reaction-video reaction. Ruby Reacts has worked herself into tears over a fake vlog and the really annoying thing is HER VIDEOS ARE JUST AS FAKE. I looked through her channel and loads of them end with her crying and saying 'I can't do this' because she's overcome with emotion. Like she feels that way every time she watches a video. Yeah right.

But I didn't record any response, of course. That would mean filming myself and watching it back, so it wouldn't be worth the pain.

FRIDAY JUNE 2ND

So what do I do with my evenings now? Emma and Callum won't be coming round anymore. I can't watch other vloggers as it will just remind me of my failure. I should get another hobby, but I can't think of anything else I want to do. Maybe I can think up some good ways to kill Sebastian.

SATURDAY JUNE 3RD

I've decided to put the whole Destiny episode behind me and start again with a new vlog. And this time I won't be misleading anyone because the star will be Loki. No one can say I'm tricking them into thinking the vlog is real, because cats don't have laptops or phones and even if they did they wouldn't be able to record videos because they don't have opposable thumbs.

I've already planned Loki's first vlog and now I'm going into the garden to gather some props.

SUNDAY JUNE 4TH

WELCOME TO MY VLOG | LOKI

Hey everyone, my name's Loki! Welcome to my first ever vlog. I'm starting off with my summer haul. I've just been into the garden and as you can see I've brought in a leaf, a chocolate-bar wrapper and a dead spider.

When you've gathered your haul, be sure to drop it at the feet of your owner and look up at them like they should be impressed.

[I used a high, silly voice for Loki. I know he wouldn't approve of this because he thinks of himself as a tough hunter, but it fitted with the footage.]

Next, I'm going to take you through my morning routine. I like to start off at around 4am, running up and down the stairs for no reason. Then at about 6am I like to wake everyone up one at a time by jumping on them.

After my morning nap, I like to scratch the back door like I want to go out, but stay inside when someone opens it. After that it's time to find a convenient place to settle, so I'll hunt around for a laptop someone is using.

This is what Loki actually does, by the way. Once, I was writing an essay and he managed to walk across my keyboard and press select all and delete. I'd like to think this was an accident, but it happened straight after I'd refused to give him some of my sandwich.

I've uploaded the video now and I'm waiting for the views to mount up. There's only been three so far, but I need to be patient. I'm sure Loki's fans are out there somewhere.

MONDAY JUNE 5TH

Emma sat next to me at lunch again today. No one teased us about the show, which was a relief.

There's a boy a few years younger called Eamonn who's been suspended for drawing on people's foreheads in permanent marker, so everyone's talking about him instead now.

I told Emma about my Loki vlog and she thought it was a good idea. She said she misses recording videos, but she's trying out for the role of Sandy in her drama group's production of Grease, so she'll be busy in the evenings again soon.

Over on the other side of the canteen, I spotted Sebastian eating an even bigger bag of cheesy puffs than usual. He better not have bought those with the profits from uploading our TV appearance. That's our misery he's crunching noisily on.

TUESDAY JUNE 6TH

Hmm. Only 20 views for Loki's vlog. Not great when you're used to view counts in the hundreds of thousands. And the only comment he's got so far is a spam link inviting him to earn over two hundred

dollars a day. That's not going to happen, unless dead
spiders are more valuable than everyone realizes.

WEDNESDAY JUNE 7TH

Great news for Emma. She got the role of Sandy in Grease, and Callum got the role of Danny. The director said they had fantastic chemistry together, and I'm taking all the credit. I'm glad Emma got something out of the vlog other than a catastrophic TV appearance and Callum got something out of it other than a French fry thrown at him by some angry girls.

THURSDAY JUNE 8TH

The Loki video has still got just 28 views and no genuine comments. I'm starting to think his vlog might not be such an amazing idea after all.

Oh well. I guess he just doesn't have the star power of Grumpy Cat, Keyboard Cat or Weird Meow Cat. It's a shame, because the only payment he'd have demanded would have been extra cat biscuits.

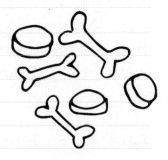

So what now? I can't bring Destiny back. But I'd like to continue vlogging somehow. I don't care about the money really, I just enjoy doing it.

FRIDAY JUNE 9TH

Today I looked back at my very first attempt at vlogging, from before I came up with the idea of Destiny. And it was just as awful as I remember. But it was only awful because I was trying to be the sort of character I thought a vlogger should be. What if I tried it again, but this time as myself? If I can be as honest in a vlog as I am here in my secret diary, people might like it. I could even call it 'The Olivia Tells The Truth Vlog'.

I still don't want to watch footage of myself back, but maybe I don't need to. I could just record the videos and upload them without editing or checking them.

I might as well do it. I've got nothing to lose.

SATURDAY JUNE 10TH

THE TRUTHFUL VLOG | OLIVIA TELLS THE TRUTH

Hi! Welcome to my channel. This is going to be just like any other vlog. Except I'll be totally honest about everything.

[I didn't shine flattering lighting on my face and I definitely didn't put makeup on. I looked like I'd got out of bed in the middle of the night to Skype a distant relative. And that's how I wanted it. There was no point in boasting about how honest the vlog was if it looked fake.]

For example, want a room tour? Too bad, my floor's covered in food wrappers, socks and books, so I can't even get across it. There's a clear path from my bed to the door and from my bed to this computer and that's pretty much it.

I went on like this for ten minutes, boasting about how lazy I am and how much I hate tidying. I uploaded it as soon as I'd finished. It might be unwatchable, but I had fun ranting at the camera anyway.

So far the video has a total of zero views, zero likes and zero dislikes. Yay! Zero dislikes! I'm the joint most popular vlogger in the world going by the lowest amount of dislikes.

SUNDAY JUNE 11TH

THE TRUTH ABOUT MY NON-EXISTENT FANS |
OLIVIA TELLS THE TRUTH

Hey everyone! Well I say 'everyone'. The view count on my last video was zero, and this one might be zero too. Hello, nobody!

It's weird, isn't it? If I sit here talking to myself it means I'm crazy. But if I sit here talking to myself and upload it, and just one person watches, it means I'm a vlogger.

When you're starting a new channel, you're meant to post links to it on the comments of other, more popular vloggers. But I'm not even going to do that. I'm enjoying the tension too much. Am I a vlogger or am I mad?

[This went on for a few minutes before I got bored and uploaded it. Two hours later, I'd had one view. I was quite pleased, but then I thought it might be Sebastian cyber-stalking me and got creeped out.]

10PM

My new video has had its first comment. It was of course spam:

> **LOL Funvids LOL**
> That video was FUN!!! For more fun videos, check out funsite.fun

I replied with, 'I must check that out. I'm looking for a fun new virus for my computer.'

I can't believe I'm arguing with spambots now. It's not

like I'm ever going to think of something so sarcastic they rise up and overthrow their programmers.

11PM

Wait, wait, wait. Stop everything. There's a real comment. Someone watched my actual video and wrote some actual words.

> **Natalie Tha Cupcake**
> I watched this! So you're not mad. Well, you are. But in a good way.

MONDAY JUNE 12TH

I was sitting with Emma in the canteen this lunchtime when the Swans walked past. Emma smiled and said hi. Jasmine and Grace bit their lips and ignored her, but Bethany scowled and said, 'We don't talk to fakers.' There's someone who's enjoying being a Swan way too much.

I don't know how she can call us fakers. Their entire clique is about being fake. All the time Emma was a Swan she did bitchy resting face whenever girls were near and flicked her hair like she was back in her milkshake commercial whenever boys were near. But she's not really like that at all. Everyone who ever joins the Swans has to pretend to be as awful as Jasmine, regardless of their true personality.

These are things I should have said to Bethany. But, like usual, all that came out was, 'Shut up.'

I spent the rest of the day feeling annoyed I hadn't said more. I was still angry when I got home, and at first I wasn't going to do a video at all. Then I decided to make it the subject of my video instead. After all, I did promise to be totally honest about what was on my mind.

THE TRUTH ABOUT THE POPULAR GANG | OLIVIA TELLS THE TRUTH

Hey, guys. Today I'm going to talk about popular cliques. Every school has that one gang who think they're better than everyone and we just accept it. Why? They just appoint themselves school royalty and the rest of us bow down like the good little servants we are.

Ooh, I can't believe the popular gang spoke to me, I feel so special! Oh I can't believe the popular gang sat next to me at lunch, it's like I'm one of them! Oh I can't believe the popular gang stole my lunch money and flushed my head down the toilet, I'm so lucky!

I went on and on until I ran out of breath. It felt great to get it all out of my system. Weirdly, I find it easier talking to a camera about this stuff than to actual people. I was worried about uploading the video in case I came across as too angry, but then I remembered no one watches anyway, so it didn't matter.

TUESDAY JUNE 13TH

I checked the vlog this morning and noticed my latest video had 134 views. That's a lot more than I was expecting. 134 more, in fact. It's hardly Destiny levels of popularity, but it's way ahead of anything Loki managed.

In your face, Loki! In your furry, whiskery face!

10PM

The view count on my vlog is at 1514 now. Not only am I more popular than my cat, I'm more popular than my mum. In the space of a day, I've risen from being the third most popular vlogger in the house to the number one spot.

There are actual comments too, from actual human non-robots, non-spammers, non-self-promoters:

MorganaEatsChocolate
<3 <3 <3 This video. Wish you were at my school
then we could sit together and laugh at the so-called
'Gorgeous Gang'. That's what the popular clique in my
school are called, by the way. Sad.

Kaylee B
There is a group just like this at our school the ringleader
is Karen and she is a cow she thinks just shes so popular
and can just take my stuff.

Clara Tha Smart Cookieee
OMG please make more I love this video. Pleeeease!
Anyway byeeee.

Evil Liam 13
I'll be honest. I came here with the intention of trolling
you. But it looks like life has already trolled you enough.

MorganaEatsChocolate
We don't care what you talk about here
#Oliviafandom

It's strange to read comments about me rather than
an imaginary character called Destiny. I thought the

trolling might be upsetting now it's about me, but I still don't really care. Those trolls are unhappy people taking out their frustrations on others. They're the outsiders at their schools — just like I am.

If anything, I feel sorry for them. Plus, when you've had a cheese-breathing goblin take revenge live on TV, a few random comments aren't going to hurt you. Positive comments, on the other hand. Now THEY'RE weird.

I get really embarrassed whenever someone says something nice in real life, even if it's just a teacher telling me they liked my essay or a relative telling me I've grown. But a stranger saying they wished I went to their school so I could be their friend is just wrong.

I feel like I might stop reading the comments on my videos soon. And if I do, it will be to avoid reading the words of the fans, not the haters. Maybe I am crazy after all.

WEDNESDAY JUNE 14TH

Charlie was watching his usual videos tonight when I tried to record my next vlog. I was worried the noise

of his laugher would be in the background, and some animal-protection officers would call round to see if we'd imprisoned a seal. I went to his room to complain, but he just turned his speakers up and laughed even louder. It doesn't even sound like real laughter anymore, he's just shouting 'ha ha ha' loud enough for my computer to pick up.

I decided the best thing would be to channel my anger into a video again:

THE TRUTH ABOUT MY BROTHER | OLIVIA TELLS THE TRUTH

Listen to that. That's my brother pretending to laugh because I just complained about the noise. Every day he watches the same five videos over and over again and giggles like he's seeing them for the first time. I asked if he could turn the sound down, so he turned it up and now he's putting on a fake laugh.

[I paused so my fans could hear the start of 'Ultimate Fail Compilation'. There was the sound of someone falling off a skateboard and screaming in pain followed by my brother shouting 'ha ha ha'.]

Why can't I have a normal brother like everyone else? Other vloggers have siblings they can do tag videos with. If I tried making a video with Charlie, he'd prod my arm and make high-pitched noises until I went into meltdown, like he does on car journeys.

[I stopped to let the noise from Charlie's room come through again. He'd forgotten all about trying to annoy me now and gone back to genuine laughter.]

That's not a seal being crammed into a blender, by the way. That's what my brother sounds like when he's laughing for real. Yes, it's unbearable living in the same house as him, thanks for asking.

I uploaded the video while I was still angry. I was a little worried the viewers might think I was mean and take pity on Charlie. But they were all on my side:

 Clara Tha Smart Cookieee
I had just come in from shouting at my idiot brother when I saw this and it cheered me up sooooo much. Anyway byeeeeeee!

Princess Amber

ROFL

> **Pedantic Penguin**
>
> … yet somehow still managing to type. I put it to you, Princess Amber, that you are not really rolling on the floor at all.

 Tangfastics Rock

Mine doesn't just laugh in an annoying way. He claps at the same time. He literally can't laugh without clapping. He's even more like a seal than yours.

MorganaEatsChocolate

That's what my brother is like too. A word of warning — if he asks you to pull his finger, don't.

Oh, Hi Jade

LOLivia

Hey Its Alicia

Why can't I have a normal brother like everyone else? Er you totally do. That's what they're like. #sad #true

THURSDAY JUNE 15TH

THE TRUTH ABOUT MY MAKEUP ROUTINE |
OLIVIA TELLS THE TRUTH

I see a lot of vloggers talking about their makeup routine. Mine won't take long to describe because I don't have one. Me and makeup just don't get on.

You watch the tutorials and they make it sound easy and then you try it and you end up sticking a mascara brush in your eye and giving yourself that attractive bloodshot look.

You make mistakes and put more on to cover them up and then make some more mistakes and you end up looking like this.

[I held up a poster of a zombie from Charlie's wall. He likes to cover his room with pictures of disgusting things just in case you're not already grossed out enough just from being there.]

So don't follow my makeup advice – ever. Unless the dead have risen from their graves and you want to disguise yourself as one and walk among them. If you want my real morning routine it's five more minutes in bed, followed by another five minutes in bed, followed by a final five minutes, followed by the real final five minutes, followed by Dad shouting.

[I switched to describing my morning snack routine after this. The video ended up being the longest one yet.]

10PM

My video about the Swans is over 4000 views, my Charlie one has topped 1000, and the makeup one isn't far behind, even though it's only been up for a couple of hours.

My makeup video must be the only one I've ever uploaded that's had no negative comments at all. I don't know if that means the trolls have finally lost interest, or if I've done their job for them by being mean about myself. Comments so far have been great:

MorganaEatsChocolate
Love these vids! Please keep making them.

Princess Amber
<3 <3 <3 Olivia

Nala Rules
I love you Olivia!!! Never stop being real!!!

People its Sarah LOL
2:32 LOL 2 THA MAX

Oh, Hi Jade
Olivia is killin it.

 Melissa Knows
You don't need makeup anyway hon. You look fab.

Kelly D
I wish I was as confident as you then I wouldn't have to wear makeup.

 Nala Rules
You don't have to wear makeup, you can do what you want. #BeMoreOlivia

FRIDAY JUNE 16TH

Dad came to my room tonight to ask if I could download him a new phone. He's asked this before and I know what he actually wants is to update the phone's software to a newer version. All you have to do is go to 'settings' and then 'check for updates', but apparently that's too much for him, because he always gets me to do it.

At least it gave me an idea for a video, which I recorded as soon as he'd gone:

THE TRUTH ABOUT MY DAD | OLIVIA TELLS THE TRUTH

Okay, so Dad just came into my room and asked me to download him a new phone. Is that because he's going to use a 3D printer to produce the different parts? No, it's because that's what he thinks installing an update is called.

How bad with technology is he? Here's one example – I once texted him to ask if he'd be home in time for dinner. He called me, said 'Yes' and hung up.

He's also convinced that LOL stands for 'Lots Of Love' instead of 'Laughing Out Loud'. I've told him a hundred times but he still can't remember. It wasn't a great way to end that text telling me my hamster had died.

Worse was the time I took him to the shops to choose a new laptop. He promised to let me do the talking, then just as we're about to pay he says, 'I think we should check if that one has Google on it.'

[I shook my head and buried it in my hands. The video went on like this, ending with the time Dad asked me to wipe the files from his monitor.]

I'm now feeling a little guilty about mocking Dad. I know he could make more effort with technology, but it's not his fault he doesn't get it. When he was growing up, computers were just for nerds. Whoever was the equivalent of Sebastian in his class would have been the only person who even had one. By the time they were everywhere, it was too late for him to catch up.

It was fun to make that video, but I don't think I'll upload it. It's not like Dad will ever see it, but I'd still feel bad putting it out there. Unlike Charlie, he hasn't really done anything to deserve it.

SATURDAY JUNE 17TH

I got a product placement offer this morning:

Hi Olivia

Allow me to introduce myself. I'm Crystal Montague from Emojearings Ltd.

Let me tell you a little bit about us, in case you haven't caught the buzz. Emojearings are high-quality earrings shaped as classic emoji such as smiley face with sunglasses and smiley pile of poo.

We're looking for up-and-coming vloggers to work with us and we think you'd be perfect. If you think so too, perhaps we could reach an agreement that works for both of us.

Crystal Montague
Managing Director and Social Media Manager
Emojearings Ltd

I wrote straight back and said I wasn't interested. I can hardly call my channel the Olivia Tells the Truth vlog and take money to push products I'd never dream of buying. The thought of just one of my viewers walking around with a golden turd on their ear would drive me mad.

I was angry they'd even contacted me. And I've learned that when I get angry, it's time to start recording.

THE TRUTH ABOUT ENDORSEMENTS | OLIVIA TELLS THE TRUTH

Hi guys. I promised to tell you the truth on this channel, so today I want to talk about a side of vlogging you don't always hear about. Because so many vloggers talk about the sort of clothes and makeup they like, they get approached by companies who pay them to mention their products. It happened to me yesterday.

[I then read out Crystal Montague's email, rolling my eyes and shaking my head. Originally I wanted to rant about what a stupid idea emoji earrings were, but then I thought Crystal might sue me, so I settled for reading the email sarcastically.]

I turned down the offer because I wouldn't wear these earrings and I don't see why you should. If you hear me endorsing anything it's because I actually like it and bought it with my own money. And seeing as though Ben & Jerry's are unlikely to approach me anytime soon, I can guarantee you won't see any product placements here.

If you're watching Ben or Jerry, my favourite flavour is chocolate fudge brownie. No? Oh well, it was worth a try.

I wish I hadn't mentioned Ben & Jerry's. I'm really craving some, but I need to wait until it goes half price again.

I wasn't sure if this glimpse behind the scenes of the vlogging world would be interesting for my fans, but they seemed to like it. The view count quickly went over 5000, and lots of comments came in:

MorganaEatsChocolate

<3 <3 <3 Loving your honesty. This is why I trust your channel.

 Melissa Knows

No one smart enough to watch your channel would buy that rubbish anyway. What are they thinking?

 Jenna D

Do they do them as nose rings too?

 Wow Subscribers

Get over a million new subscribers instantly for a great price increasefollowers.com/redirect/1782436170

 Hey Its Alicia

Thumbs up if you were an original Olivia fan before EVERYONE got into her.

 Evil Liam 13

Thumbs up if you're an annoying hipster who needs to get back to the organic juice bar.

 Hey Its Alicia

Whatever dude I liked her before EVERYONE else, deal with it haterz.

SUNDAY JUNE 18TH

I saw Charlie coming home with a shopping trolley this afternoon. He wouldn't say what it was for, but I saw he'd tried to set up a channel of his own called 'Dare Charlie' where he promised to take on any dare, no matter how dangerous. It had only been viewed 152 times, but he already had a few comments:

 Wacky Waving Inflatable Imran
Ride a shopping trolley down some stairs.

 Dan the Mansplainer
Go to the furniture store and use a display toilet for real. We're talking number twos here, not just pee.

 Troll Express
Eat a tin of cat food without barfing.

 James Flames
Light a firecracker and throw it down your parents' toilet.

 Dominic The Insane
Wake up your family with an air horn in the night.

Was Charlie planning on working his way through all these? If so, I'm glad I discovered it in time. If the first dares hadn't killed him, the last one definitely would have done.

I showed his video to Mum and Dad and he's been grounded for a month. But rather than thanking me for saving his life and, more importantly, our toilet, they got angry with me for putting the idea of vlogging into his head.

Vlogs have nothing to do with it. Idiots will always find ways to do stupid stuff. The day after shopping carts were invented some fool probably rode one down a staircase. If Charlie had really been copying me, he'd have made an intelligent video and attracted awesome subscribers rather than idiots who want him to injure himself for their amusement.

MONDAY JUNE 19TH

My week got off to the worst possible start. Did Charlie actually go through with the air horn dare? Did I fall down a sinkhole? Did I wake up convinced it was the weekend?

Worse — Sebastian returned to my life. I've done such a good job of avoiding him since the TV show, I almost forgot he existed.

This morning he was waiting outside the school gates with a crumpled piece of paper. He shoved it towards me and said he was offering to be my agent. He said he was pleased to see I'd started an honest vlog and that it was great to see someone telling the complete truth about absolutely everything they'd ever done.

This was of course a threat. He was saying that unless I signed, he'd tell my new fans about the whole Destiny thing. No doubt he was planning to post the link to our TV disaster to every video I ever made.

I ripped up his contract and walked off without saying anything.

Now I'm worrying about Cheese Breath's threat. I've given up on the New York trip, so it doesn't really matter if I agree to give him half of whatever money I make from the new channel. But it's the principle. I can't let him win.

9PM

I just got an email from Crystal Montague thanking me for promoting Emojearings and telling me she got a 'totally amazeballs spike in traffic' after my video.

Really? I openly criticize her earrings and still she thanks me. Goes to show there's no such thing as bad publicity.

That could be a pretty good angle, I suppose. I could charge companies to bitch about their products, knowing everyone will buy them anyway.

I'm tempted to ask Crystal if I can have the money I turned down, seeing as though she got her traffic spike anyway. But then I'd have to admit it in my honest vlog, so it wouldn't be worth it.

TUESDAY JUNE 20TH

Sebastian came over to me in the canteen this lunchtime and said his offer was still on. In other words, I need to employ him as my 'agent' soon or he'd tell the fans about Destiny.

I made up my mind about what to do straight away.

THE TRUTH ABOUT ME | OLIVIA TELLS THE TRUTH

When I started this vlog, I said I'd be as honest as I could. But I didn't explain why that was so important for me.

The truth is that earlier this year I started a vlog called The Destiny Channel. I wrote the words for the videos, but got my friend Emma to read them out. Some people thought this was dishonest and I was confronted about it on a TV show. After that, I deleted the channel and started this vlog instead.

Today the same boy who confronted me on that show, Sebastian, has threatened to tell you I was behind the Destiny vlog.

So I'm telling you myself. There you go, Sebastian. You can't threaten to tell everyone because I've already done it myself. Now go and find someone else to blackmail.

I uploaded this video tonight and waited for the comments to come in. I had prepared myself in advance and was ready to delete the channel if things turned sour. But it didn't happen.

If anything, this new video was more popular than the others. It even looks like the old Destiny fans have finally managed to find my new channel. I recognized a few of their names in the comment section:

Poppy M
Love your videos, please keep making them.

DestinyMonster02
2:17 That guy: Ew …

xxFashionGirlxx
OMG I love this video we are so alike.

destinyisperfect
This channel is soooooooooooooooooooooooooooooooooo
ooooooooooooooo perfect.

It was great to see these old names again. And it
gave me an idea for the next video.

WEDNESDAY JUNE 21ST

I deliberately hadn't included any links to
Sebastian's channel in my last video, as I didn't
want to feel like I was setting my fans on him. But
one of them posted this comment:

 DestinyMonster02
I've found the channel of the creep who tried to blackmail
Olivia. Let's all go there and school the fool. bit.ly/1VTAOcO

A few minutes later, comments were piling up
underneath Sebastian's latest gaming video.

DatFreakyGrrl
Threatening people sucks. This channel sucks. You suck.

Poppy M
Thumbs up if you think Sebastian is a loser.

SHOUTING LAUREN
SO MANY THUMBS

xxFashionGirlxx
OMG we are so not alike.

destinyisperfect
Sebastian is soooo not perfect.

Evil Liam 13
Thanks to whoever sent me to this channel. I will have fun.

Sebastian didn't respond to any of the comments, but I saw him wincing at his phone in the lunch hall, so I'm sure he's seen them.

Despite everything Sebastian has done to me, I felt a little sorry for him. I won't mention him again, and hopefully the fans will forget about him. I don't want

*to be the ringleader of an angry mob, even if he
did try to blackmail me and ruin my life.*

THURSDAY JUNE 22ND

OLIVIA'S TRUTH VLOG INTRODUCES EMMA |
OLIVIA TELLS THE TRUTH

Hi everyone. I've got a very special guest star
today. It's my best friend Emma. Ta-dah!

Emma is an actress and she's in my class,
and she appeared on my last channel too,
as some of you may remember. She'll be
starring in *Grease* soon, but she's going to pop
in for challenges between rehearsals.

Today it's the marshmallow challenge. We both have
to stuff our mouths full and try to describe
something. It could be a film or a TV show or a book,
anything really.

[At this point I opened a bag of marshmallows and

we shoved them into our mouths. The rest of the video was pretty much us going 'MMMMM UUUUGHHH MMMMM' and giggling.]

Even though I made it as clear as possible that Emma was not Destiny, the fans took no notice. As far as they're concerned, their heroine has returned. Oh well. At least no one can accuse me of misleading them this time.

 Chloe C
OMG Destiny is back. I'm so happy I want to cry.

 They Call Me Super Jennifer
Olivia and Destiny in the same video = best crossover ever.

 Clara Tha Smart Cookieee
Hi! Blindfold makeup challenge next. Pleeeease! Byeeee.

 xxFashionGirlxx
OMG you have a best friend too Destiny. We are so alike.

 SHOUTING LAUREN
DESTINY!!!!!!!!!!!!!!!!!!!!!!!!!!!!! YAY

Evil Liam 13
Love what you've done with your hair since the last time we saw you, Destiny. The way you've combed it over your top lip is amazing.

destinyisperfect
Shut up Destiny and Olivia are flawless #Fandom #Perfection

Wildcat Katherine
Destiny and Olivia BFF. Epic.

The Justine Rodriguez Show
Anyone who disliked this LEAVE EARTH NOW.

Poppy M
Destiny Fam are back!!!

I can hardly blame the fans for getting confused. Emma's much more like Destiny since she left the Swans. She's even stopped doing bitchy rest face. I used to notice her switch into friendly mode when I started filming, but now she's like that all the time.

FRIDAY JUNE 23RD

Jasmine came over at lunch today and I braced myself for whatever insult she had lined up. But I could never have prepared for what she actually said.

Apparently one of her cousins sent her a link to my channel. Now she's found out I'm popular online she wants me to, get this, JOIN THE SWANS.

I was actually speechless. Jasmine said that she knew it must be a shock, but I really was popular enough to be accepted into their gang.

What part of 'I hate bitchy popular cliques' doesn't she understand? I can hardly make a video mocking her gang one minute and join the next. How would my next video go? 'Sorry I was wrong, popular gangs are awesome really and you're all a bunch of nerdy losers'?

Instead of saying anything, I stared out of the window and blanked her. Loads of people stopped to watch as she clicked her fingers in my face and said, 'Hello?' I tried really hard to do bitchy resting face, but I ended up laughing.

No doubt she'll try and get back at me. But when she does, I'll just make a video about her. And that's why you don't mess with a vlogger.

SATURDAY JUNE 24TH

My online fame must have spread to my old school. Yesterday I got a text message from Jess saying how totally awesome my vlog was and asking why I didn't tell her about it. Er, because she didn't reply to my last five messages and I thought she wasn't interested in me anymore.

Now Sam, Han and even Steph have also miraculously remembered my number and texted me.

It's all very strange. View counts are just numbers on a screen, but they have magic powers. They can make bitchy cliques decide you're cool enough and they can make people from your old school suddenly remember they're friends with you.

I'll get round to replying to their texts eventually, but I won't do it right away. Emma's got a night off from rehearsals, so she's coming round to record a whisper challenge.

10PM

BIG news. Emma's going out with Callum in real life now!

screams and fans face

That's better.

When Emma arrived I asked her how rehearsals for *Grease* were going, and she kept blushing. I knew something was up, but it took me ages to get the truth out of her.

Apparently Callum broke up with his old girlfriend Megan a couple of weeks ago. Things haven't been the same between them since a group of angry girls accused him of being a cheater and threw fries at them.

I'd like to say I reacted in a mature and supportive way, but the truth is I blasted 'Summer Nights' out of my speakers while Emma sank on to my bed with her head in her hands.

It's strange. Since I deleted the vlog, Emma has become much more like Destiny and now she's actually going out with Callum. If I'd kept it going it wouldn't even be that fake anymore. Definitely weird.

FRIDAY JULY 21ST

I've been so busy with my channel that I'd forgotten all about this diary. I've just realized I haven't updated it for almost a month.

I record a video every day now. Whether there's something I want to get off my chest or I just want to tell everyone how bored I am. Some take off and some don't. It's hard to predict.

My most popular video, currently on 573,573 views and rising, is one where I list facts about myself, such as my favourite chocolate bars and music. I have no idea why that went viral. I tried to watch it back to see if I accidentally said something clever, but I still can't stand looking at myself on screen so I gave up.

Another that seems popular is one about my failed attempt to start a vlog for Loki. I linked to his original video in the description, and even that's had over 50,000 views now. I bought him a fuzzy

pink mouse stuffed with catnip to celebrate but he soon reduced it to fluffy roadkill. But, honestly, I'm sort of glad the Loki vlog didn't work. It's a nightmare directing a star that naps for practically the whole day.

I've even been invited to The International Vlogging Conference in Seattle next month. They've asked me to take part in a panel calling 'Finding Your Vlogging Voice'. Seeing as though I'm there to promote the Olivia Tells the Truth vlog, I should tell the truth and say I just talk into the camera and upload it. But that won't take long, and I don't have any other skills to

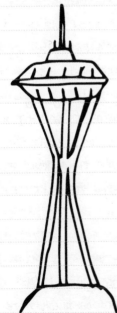

entertain the crowd, so I'd better prepare a bit more.

It took me ages to get permission to go. In the end I had to agree to let Dad come too, though he's promised not to attempt to talk to anyone about techie stuff. I also told Mum I'd mention her channel to all the fans. And I will, if someone asks what the worst vlog I've ever seen is.

The organizers are paying for my flight and hotel, but they couldn't afford to cover Emma's costs too. She's a regular guest on my vlog now, so I thought the fans would be upset if they couldn't meet her. Then two days ago I got an ad revenue payment that was enough to pay for her flight and hotel, so now she can come along too. I just hope she doesn't spend the whole time going on and on about Callum. Yeah I'm happy for them, but it gets boring.

The school trip to New York is happening this week. It's weird to think how desperate I was to go. Now it's come round I don't care about it at all. I've got my mind on much more exciting things.

It still doesn't seem real. After trying so hard to make vlogs about a perky fashion-lover and a disgruntled cat, the most successful one turned out to be me, staring at my computer, saying whatever came into my head.

But that's the great thing about vlogging. Whoever you are, whatever you're like, there may be thousands out there just like you. Maybe hundreds of thousands. And they might want to listen to what you've got to say. To find out, all you have to do is record and upload.